SEEING RED

SEEING RED

—

Lina Meruane

TRANSLATED FROM THE SPANISH BY
MEGAN McDOWELL

atlantic·*fiction*

First published as *Sangre en el ojo* in Chile in 2012 by Pangea Libros.

First published in the United States of America in 2016
by Deep Vellum Publishing, Texas.

First published in hardback in Great Britain in 2017 by Atlantic Books,
an imprint of Atlantic Books Ltd.

This paperback edition published in Great Britain in 2018 by Atlantic Books.

1 2 3 4 5 6 7 8 9

A CIP catalogue record for this book is available from the British Library.

Paperback ISBN: 978 1 786 493 156
E-Book ISBN: 978 1 786 493 149

Printed in Great Britain by Clays Ltd, St Ives plc
Atlantic Books
An Imprint of Atlantic Books Ltd.
Ormond House
26–27 Boswell Street
London
WC1N 3JZ

www.atlantic-books.co.uk

To Paul,
keeping watch in the darkness

I raised my head in horror and saw Lina staring at me with black, glassy, motionless eyes. A smile, between loving and ironic, creased my beloved's lips. I jumped up in desperation and grabbed Lina roughly by the hand.

"What have you done, you wretched woman?"

CLEMENTE PALMA, *Los ojos de Lina* (Lina's Eyes)

burst

It was happening. Right then, happening. They'd been warning me for a long time, and yet. I was paralyzed, my sweaty hands clutching at the air, while the people in the living room went on talking, roaring with laughter—even their whispers were exaggerated, while I. And someone shouted louder than the rest, turn the music down, don't make so much noise or the neighbors'll call the cops at midnight. I focused in on that thundering voice that never seemed to tire of repeating that even on Saturdays the neighbors went to bed early. Those *gringos* weren't night owls like us, party people to the core. Good protestant folks who would indeed protest if we kept them from their sleep. On the other side of the walls, above our bodies and under our feet, too, these *gringos*—so used to greeting dawn with their socks on and shoes already tied—were restless. *Gringos* who sat down in their impeccable underwear and ironed faces to eat their breakfasts of cereal with cold milk. But none of us were worried about those sleepless *gringos*, their heads buried under pillows, their throats stuffed with pills that would bring no relief as long as we kept trampling their rest. If the people in the living room went on trampling, that is, not me. I was still in the bedroom, kneeling, my arm stretched out toward the floor. In that instant, precisely, in that half-light, in that commotion, I found myself thinking about the neighbors' oppressive sleeplessness, imagining them as they turned out the

3

lights after stuffing earplugs in their ears, how they'd push them in so hard the silicone would burst. I thought I would much rather have been the one with broken earplugs, the one with eardrums pierced by shards. I would rather have been the old woman resolutely placing the mask over her eyelids, only to yank it off again and switch on the light. I wished for that while my still-suspended hand encountered nothing. There was only the alcoholic laughter coming through the walls and spattering me with saliva. Only Manuela's strident voice yelling over the noise for the umpteenth time, Come on, guys, keep it down a little. No, please don't, I said to myself, keep talking, keep shouting, howl, growl if you must. Die laughing. That's what I said to myself, my body seized up though only a few seconds had passed. I'd only just come into the master bedroom, just leaned over to search for my purse and the syringe. I had to give myself an injection at twelve o'clock sharp but now I wouldn't make it, because the pile of precariously balanced coats let my purse slide to the floor, because instead of stopping conscientiously, as I should have, I bent over and reached to pick it up. And then a firecracker went off in my head. But no, it was no fire I was seeing, it was blood spilling out inside my eye. The most shockingly beautiful blood I have ever seen. The most outrageous. The most terrifying. The blood gushed, but only I could see it. With absolute clarity I watched as it thickened, I saw the pressure rise, I watched as I got dizzy, I saw my stomach turn, saw that I was starting to retch, and even so. I didn't straighten up or move an inch, didn't even try to breathe while I watched the show. Because that was the last thing I would see, that night, through that eye: a deep, black blood.

dark blood

There would be no more admonitions impossible to follow. Stop smoking, first of all, and then don't hold your breath, don't cough, do not for any reason pick up heavy packages, boxes, suitcases. Never ever lean over, or dive headfirst into water. The carnal throes of passion were forbidden, because even an ardent kiss could cause my veins to burst. They were brittle, those veins that sprouted from my retina and coiled and snaked through the transparent humor of my eye. To observe the growth of that winding vine of capillaries and conduits, to keep watch day by day over its millimetric expansion. That was the only thing that could be done: keep watch over the sinuous movement of the venous web advancing toward the center of my eye. That was all and it was a lot, the optician declared, just that, that's it, he would repeat, averting his eyes and looking at my clinical history that had grown into a mountain of papers, a thousand-page manuscript stuffed into a manila folder. Knitting his graying eyebrows, Lekz wrote the precise biography of my retinas, their uncertain prognosis. Then he cleared his throat and subjected me to the details of new research protocols. At one point he dropped the phrase transplants in experimental stages. Only I didn't qualify for any experiments: I was either too young, or my veins too thick, or the procedure too risky. We had to wait until the results were published in specialized journals, and for the government to approve new drugs. Time also stretched out like arbitrary veins, and the eye doctor went on talking nonstop, ignoring my impatience. And what if there's a hemorrhage, doctor, I was saying, clenching his protocols between my teeth. But it didn't bear thinking about, he said; better not to think at all, he said, better to just keep an eye on it and take some notes that would be impossible to decipher later on. But soon he would raise his eyes from his illegible calligraphy to concede that if it happened, if it came to pass, if in fact the event occurred, then we would have to see. Then *you'll* see, I muttered, holed up in my hate: I hope you can catch a glimpse of something then, once I no longer can. And now it had happened. I no longer saw anything but blood in one eye. How long would before the other one broke? This was finally the blind alley, the dark passage where only anonymous, besieged cries could be heard. But no, maybe not, I thought, getting hold of myself, sitting down on the coats in that bedroom of Manuela's, folding my toes inward while my shoes swung like corpses. No, I told myself, because with my eyes already broken I would dance again, jump again, kick doors open with no risk of bleeding out; I could jump off the balcony, bury the blade of an open pair of scissors between my eyebrows. Become the master of the alley, or find the way out. That's what I thought without thinking, fleetingly. I started to ransack the drawers in search of a forgotten pack of cigarettes and a lighter. I was going to burn my fingernails lighting the cigarette, fill myself with tobacco before returning to that doctor's office and saying to him, the smoke now risen to my head, tell me what you see now, doctor, tell me, coldly, urgently, strangled by resentment, as if his gloved hands had wrenched my sick eye out by its roots: tell me now, tell me whatever you want, because now he couldn't tell me anything. It was Saturday night or more like Sunday, and there was no way to get in touch with the doctor. And in any case, what could he say that I didn't already know: liters of rage were clouding my vision?

that face

As I put out the cigarette and straightened up, I saw a thread of blood run across my other eye. A fine thread that immediately started to dissolve. Soon it would be nothing but a dark spot, but it was enough to turn the air around me murky. I opened the door and stopped to look at what remained of the night: just a pasty light coming from what must be the living room, shadows moving to the rhythm of a murderous music. Drums. Rock chords. Discordant voices. There would be appetizers languishing on the table, and potato chips, a dozen beers. The ashtrays must still be only half-full, I thought, without actually seeing them. The party stayed its course and no one had any intention of stopping it. If only the wide-awake *gringos* would start banging on the walls with their broomsticks, I thought. If only the cops would come and make us turn off the music, put away all that old Argentine rock, pick up the trays with stony faces. If only they would make us put our shoes on, toss back the last dregs in the bottles, tell the last tired joke, hurry through the goodbyes and see-you-laters. But the early morning still stretched out ahead of us. Of me. Of Ignacio, who was still indiscernible in the fog. Ignacio would understand the situation without my needing to say get me out of here, take me home. I was sure his panting exhaustion would come to my rescue, his finger poking my cheek. Why so serious?, he said, suddenly beside me. Hearing his voice shattered my composure, dashed it to the floor as he added: Why the long face? And how was I to know what kind of face I had, when I'd misplaced my lips and my mole, when even my earlobes had gotten lost. All I had left were a couple of blind eyes. And I heard myself saying, Ignacio,

7

chirping Ignacio like a bird, Ignacio, I'm bleeding, this is the blood and it's so dark, so awfully thick. But no. That wasn't what I said, but rather, Ignacio, I think I'm bleeding again, why don't we go. Go? he said (you said it, Ignacio, that's what you said even though now you deny it, and then you fell silent). And I heard him ask if it was a lot of blood, maybe assuming it was like so many other times, just a bloody particle that quickly dissolved in my humors. Not so much, no, I lied, but let's go. Let's go now. But no. Let's wait until the party winds down, till the conversation dies of its own accord. Let's not be the ones to kill it, as if it weren't already dead. We'e leave in a little while, and what's an hour more or half an hour less when there's no longer anything ahead. I could drink another glass of wine and anesthetize myself, another glass of wine and get drunk. (Yes, pour me another glass, I whispered, while you filled it up with blood.) And I drank to the health of my parents, who were snoring miles away from the disaster, to the health of my friends' uproar, to the health of the neighbors who hadn't complained about the noise, the health of the medics who never came to my rescue, to the motherfucking health of health.

stumbling along

And we all left the party together, saying nothing but thanks, see you later, bye; and I guess the group gradually scattered along the way, because I can't see them in my memory. The elevator was full of voices, but when we went outside there were only three or four bodies, and then only one walking next to me. Julián was telling me about his job talk at the university or who knows what, while I moved deeper into unprecedented darkness. Ignacio would be behind us, talking his Spanish politics with Arcadio, or maybe he'd gone off to hunt for a taxi. At that hour, on that scrawny island wedged in next to Manhattan, it wouldn't be easy to find a cab. We'd have been more likely to come across an abandoned wheelchair with a loose spring. A chair would have helped me, made me less vulnerable to the night's uncertainty. A chair, so much better than a cumbersome cane. And I thought back to that very afternoon when we'd crossed over the river in the tramway along with a dozen people, variously maimed, in their wheel-chairs. Roosevelt was an island of wheelchairs where only a few professors and students lived, and no tourists came; it was a poor, protected island that almost no one visited, I thought, thinking next that I should have realized why I'd ended up traveling with all those people beside me, them and me all the same hanging above the waters. On the shore stood Fate and he was raising a question, an admonition. What did you come here looking for? he said, pointing one finger. What did you lose on this island? A chair, I answered, outside of time and circumstance, just a metal chair, with wheels, with pedals and levers and maybe even a button to propel it forward. If only you'd had a little more foresight, you would have your chair, answered my dour inner voice. At least you'd have one for tonight, when you were going to need it. But now the maimed would all be sleeping soundly, with their chairs disabled and parked next to their beds. Mine, my bed, which wasn't mine but rather Ignacio's, was still far away. Everything seemed far from me now, and getting ever farther. Ignacio had disappeared and Julián quickened his pace, spurred on by the beers. I was inevitably

9

being left behind. I moved in slow motion, sliding over the slippery gravel, plummeting off curbs, stumbling over steps. Julián must have come back when he realized he was talking to himself, I felt him supporting me by the elbow and saying fizzily, "I'd better help you, looks like you're a bit drunk, too." He started to laugh at me and I also started shaking in an attack of panic and booming laughter. And in that laughter or those convulsions Julián dragged me forward, interrogating me, did my feet hurt?, were my knees stuck?, because, *joder*, he said Spanishly, why the hell are you going so slow? I kept walking with my eyes fixed on the ground as if that would save me from falling, and with my head sunk miserably between my shoulders I tried to explain what was happening: I left my glasses at home, I can't see anything. Glasses! And since when do you wear glasses? You've kept that nice and hidden! he exclaimed, wasted and dead tired. And warning me that we were walking through a stretch of wet grass, he went on repeating, I can't believe it! You never wear glasses! Never, it was true. I had never bought a pair of glasses. Until twelve o'clock that night I'd had perfect vision. But by three o'clock Sunday morning, even the most powerful magnifying glass wouldn't have helped me. Raising his voice and maybe also his finger, like the university professor he would become, Julián brandished his ragged tongue to chastise me. You get what you deserve. And, swallowing or spitting saliva, he announced that the price of my vanity would be to trudge through life, forever stumbling.

LINA MERUANE

tomorrow

(There I am. There I go. Looking out again through the taxi
window, staring, trying to grab hold of some bit of the horizon
from the highway, the hollowed silhouette of the two pulverized
towers, the line of the mutilated sky beside the fragile glow of the
star-splashed river, the History Channel neon dazzling above the
water. I see it all without seeing it; I see it from the memory of
having seen it or through your eyes, Ignacio. The taxi's headlights
sliced through a light nocturnal fog of paper and charred metal
that refused to dissipate, that adhered to the glass as condensation.
Our driver shoved his way in, cutting off other cars, but he also
let others pass him, speeding and honking their horns. You two
were dozing and maybe you even fell asleep, rocked by the sharp
acceleration and violent braking. I settled my forehead against the
window and closed my eyes until your voice shook me, Ignacio,
a voice so new in my life I sometimes take a second to recognize
it, a voice that also changed tone when you shifted into another
language. Your voice was giving instructions in English to the taxi
driver: get off at the next exit, cross over to the west, toward the
Washington Bridge still ablaze on the horizon. We hadn't planned
on crossing that iron bridge, we weren't heading for the suburb
on the other side where I had once lived and had no intention of
returning. I was throwing myself into the present, the only thing
I had as we dropped Julián off on the corner where his building
was and continued on toward yours, which was now ours. And
as soon as we were alone, you took my face in your hands and
turned it so I'd look at you. So you could look at me. Your eyes saw
nothing extraordinary, they didn't see what lay behind my pupils.

II

Was it a lot? Much more than ever before, I told you somberly, but maybe tomorrow. Tomorrow you'll be better. But tomorrow was already today: it only had to grow light, the failing streetlights had only to be eclipsed by the sun. Turban-crowned, the driver stopped abruptly and we slid forward. Don't move, you said, and then I heard the door slam, and you must have circled around to open the door for me, to give me your hand, warn me to duck my head. From far away, anyone would have thought we were emerging from another era, not a car. We got out of the time machine arm in arm and went up the stairs the same way, toward the elevator and the five floors up. We went arm in arm down the hall until the jangling of keys in the lock. The apartment's stale air received us. The heat rose from every corner, from the floor now carpetless, from the utterly bare walls, the countless boxes that seemed full of smoldering embers instead of books. We'd spent days packing for our imminent move. I went straight down the hallway to the bedroom and you followed behind: watch out, I'm leaving a glass of water for you here. And we threw ourselves onto the bed and in spite of the humidity we embraced and, oily from sweat, we slept. And the next morning you raised the blinds and sat down beside me, waiting for me to wake up from either my sleep or my life. But I'd been wide awake for hours, not daring to open my eyes. Lucina? I raised an eyelid and then the other and to my astonishment there was light, a bit of light, enough light: the bloody shadow hadn't disappeared from my right eye, but the one in the left had sunk to the bottom. I was only half blind. And so I accepted your coffee and raised it to my lips without hesitation, and I even smiled, because, in spite of everything. And you

were there, and it was as if you were one-eyed, too, you couldn't
understand what had happened. You couldn't calculate the gravity.
You couldn't bring yourself to ask all the questions. You balled
them up and stuffed them, like now, in your pockets.)

a beat-up truck

Only a few days until the eye doctor comes back from his con-
ference and sees the terminal state of my retinas. Maybe Friday.
It's only Tuesday. Three days during which we have to resolve the
rest of our lives. Tomorrow we will stop being tenants, and we'll
settle into an apartment Ignacio will spend the next thirty years
paying for. We were moving only a few blocks east, where the
neighborhood descends stairs and elevators to meet synagogues
and tall hats, sidelocks, synthetic wigs, long black robes, where
old orthodox and archaic young Jews share the corner with the
Dominican clamor. We were going to live at that hinge: our window to the south, the door framing the north. We talked about
nothing but the move and its details, we held ourselves strictly
to the concrete, to moving ourselves immediately toward the
future. Toward the moment when we pushed the thick wooden
door and turned the doorknob. When we breathed in the smell
of fresh paint and turpentine, varnish, and sawdust still hanging
in the air. We would verify that every repair had been duly made
in that apartment whose previous owners had gradually destroyed
it. It was imperative to still have an eye, one eye at least to be sure
that everything was ok, a sharp eye to make up for a blind one.
Because the only seeing eye that I still had was no longer sighted

when I moved: my coming and going roiled the blood pooled
in my retina, agitated it like a feather duster; the push broom of
my movement churned it up. But there was no time for stillness,
and I threw myself compulsively into packing. Ignacio went out
in search of more empty boxes, while I stowed our clothes in
suitcases, stuffed our shoes and boots into enormous plastic bags,
put the plates between the sheets and our only blanket, the salad
bowls between towels. All by touch. I wrapped mugs and cups
in newspaper until finally it was Wednesday and a beat-up truck
appeared on the corner. It was noon, three guys were at the door.
They wore faces pressed for time and they carried with them
six hands full of fingers. A tall and thin black man gave orders
to another one, too young and very short, who was teamed up
with the biggest of them all: a muscular and perhaps somewhat
retarded white guy. (You told me about him, terrified, when you
returned from the first floor.) He needed direction, the muscular
guy, because he regularly pounded the hallway walls, the doorways,
the molding, windowpanes, doorjambs, the roof of the diminutive
elevator in which he almost didn't fit. On the second trip down,
the old elevator started to falter; it died on the mezzanine floor,
and that guy, the muscular one, was the only one who could lift
the mattress on his shoulders. And the bed frame. And the heavy
work table and then nine shelves. More books than we would ever
read. And also the ones I'd published under a pen name and the
manuscript of an inconclusive novel that maybe now I'd never
finish, I thought, swallowing my anguish without pausing to chew
it. Too much paper and so little furniture. We didn't have much,
but even so it was a lot for one man. So what should have taken

us a couple of hours ended up taking four or maybe five. And when everything was finally in the truck, the elevator unfroze and I could go down with the shopping cart carrying the things we'd hidden from the men. The old TV, the radio, two laptops; some half-drunk bottles of liquor and the glasses we'd use to celebrate that very night. You take it over, I don't trust these guys to be careful. Can you? Of course I can, I half-lied. I can do it perfectly well. They got into the truck to drive down the few blocks separating one building from the other, taking turns pushing because the battery was failing, and then I forgot about them. I lifted my nose to follow the smell of wet cement from some neighbor who must be watering. I felt my way to turn left, and I headed off very slowly in search of the subway station.

shopping cart move

The route I knew no longer coincided with my steps. I couldn't distinguish streetlights from trees in that murky tide, I couldn't be sure they were cars I distinguished next to the possible park on the corner. I moved along like a disoriented bat, following intuitions. I followed behind the people who passed me. If they stopped I stopped too; if they crossed a street, I caught up to them with my cart squealing metallically. I rode the elevator down to the oppressive subway station and skirted the turnstiles to make for the long corridor, until I found the exit leading to our new neighborhood. No one seemed to be ahead of me, or behind me. No rigorous rabbis to ask for directions or old ladies with backs bent over their walkers. No old person with flailing cane I could assault with my uncertainty. I slipped through the heavy station doors, and I stopped to train my ear to a bicycle crossing puddles, the slow turning of a car parking in reverse, the sporadic horns honking, the avenue's green lights. The street wasn't a place, it was a crowd of sounds all elbowing and shoving. And there was the whisper of a rotten gutter. Garbage bags piled up in the street, chafing against the breeze. A clamor of birds being electrocuted on the wires. Children shouting and chasing each other. Enough, I told myself, because it was vital that I find the sidewalk's edge. The bottles clanked loudly against each other as I bumped down, and they hit each other again as the cart bounced in potholes and grated against the curb. I raised the front wheels and then the back and I set off again on my bumpy ride. I put my neurons and their bristly dendrites to work on the math of the steps that should take me from one corner to the other. Eighty to the first and turn right. Eighty, left. Right, eighty-nine. And I was almost there. I felt the warm air churning my hair and cooling my face. I must have been close to the entrance to the building when I heard a voice's hey, its sharp and energetic, what's up. I stopped. Who could this woman be, in that neighborhood, on that street, at dusk? Who, when I was a new arrival to that intersection? I raised my face with the hint of a meticulous smile of hate, insulting through my teeth all those musicians with perfect hearing, the leathery telephone operators, the blind from birth who are trained to recognize voices. I cursed that woman but also myself for smiling at her with my whole body, with my stupid lips pronouncing a hi there all soaked in saliva. There I was, alone before that voice that assaulted and penetrated my person. The voice kept coming closer, throwing words and some kind of perfume while she, the voice, but especially the sharp shoes, their heels drumming against the cement, said something that the wail of an ambulance kept me from understanding. And then the footsteps moved away. And the perfume began to dissipate. And the woman went on talking with someone submerged far away, inside her phone.

no light bulbs

Ignacio pounced on me as I entered. They just left, he exclaimed. It's full of boxes, but come see how the repairs turned out. He dragged me by the hand like a child while I tried not to crash into the walls of the narrow hallway. In a minute he had taken me to see the refinished floor of the living room, the newly painted bedroom, the splendors of the kitchen, the shadowy bathroom that we'd leave for another day when we had more money. The apartment felt colossal, and to judge by Ignacio's eyes (to judge by the memory of your eyes, which are also mine) it still felt uninhabited. We had almost nothing and nearly all of it was his, and we'd decided to bring only what was indispensable. Everything else was so worn out, so collected from streets and subways, so abandoned on curbs or stolen from lives that came before ours. Leave the past where it had perished instead of lugging it with us to that newly remodeled apartment. There's nowhere to sit, cautioned Ignacio as if excusing himself, but we'll get some beach chairs and put them in the living room. I answered that yes, of course, whatever you want, while thinking what do you mean? We'll buy a sofa and a recliner and a pair of chairs and splendid lamps. But first we'll paint again to cover all the sickly white on the walls. We'll have to get to work soon, I thought, tomorrow if possible. There were only two days left before the eye doctor's dreaded news, but we showered happily without a curtain, washing our hair with whatever was at hand. And we put on the same clothes, sweaty but now dry, and we sat on the newly sanded and varnished floor. Look what they did, said Ignacio. It's too dark, I said. True, he replied, grabbing my hand and guiding one of my fingers to slide along the rough groove, full of splinters, that went across the room. They dragged the bookshelf here, he continued dryly; all the way to here, sorrowfully; the whole length of the room, with something like resigned rage. I saw him coming but I couldn't stop him, he went on, and I imagined the muscular man's strong but soft arms, covered by a barely-there, transparent down, his punished-dog eyes, the stupefied muteness of the man who had ruined our floor. But what could a little scratch in the wood matter to us? We'd lay a rug over it. Then we'd lay each other on top of that scratch and the Persian rug I'd pick out once I had eyes again. And once we finished getting laid, exhausted but radiant and satisfied, we'd start all over again. We'd screw like animals on every scratch the house had, in every hole in the wall, like insects. I thought of the scrapes and homemade defects that we'd leave on the house, that we'd collect gradually, maybe. I was worry-free as I stretched out on the floor with my eyes shut tight. Ignacio uncorked a bottle in the kitchen and complained, his voice becoming abstract, where'd you put the glasses, where'd you put the napkins, opening and closing crates and rummaging in boxes. I got lost in the crackle of newspaper between his fingers, in the cork that shot against the wall, and the champagne fizz. Because that was the only certainty: inaugurating our life with glasses washed by shadow, letting ourselves be stunned by the silence. It was night already and we didn't have electricity, there wasn't a single bare lightbulb swinging from the sockets. Not even a candle. Ignacio had no clue where the lighter was. He searched through clothes and felt his way over the floor, looking for it but not finding it. And we also toasted to that, because in the darkness of the empty house we were the same: a couple of blind lovers.

house of hard knocks

Thwacks against half-closed doors, all of their edges blunt. A nose mashed against a shelf. Scratched fingers, broken nails, twisted ankles almost sprained. Ignacio took note of every mishap and tried to clear the boxes still only half-emptied, he moved the open bags from the hallway and cleared away orphan shoes, but then I got tangled up in rugs, I knocked over posters leaning against walls, I toppled trash cans. I was buried in open boxes with table legs between my fingers. The house was alive, it wielded its doorknobs and sharpened its fixtures while I still clung to corners that were no longer where they belonged. It changed shape, the house, the rooms castled, the furniture swapped places to confuse me. With one eye blind with blood and the other clouded over at my every movement, I was lost, a blindfolded chicken, dizzy and witless. But I dried some sheepish tears and counted my steps again, memorizing: five long steps to the living room and eight short ones back to the bedroom, kitchen to the left, ten to the bathroom, to the left. The windows must be somewhere and I bumped right into Ignacio. You're dangerous, he told me, angry, trying not to yell at me; stop wandering around, we'll end up breaking all our bones. I know he stood there looking at me because I felt his eyes on mine, like snails coating me in their slime. Lina, he sighed, immersed in a sudden sadness or shyness. Lina, now even softer, holding my chin, his slimy eyes everywhere: you're blind, you're blind and dangerous. Yes, I replied, slowly. Yes, but I'm only an apprentice blind woman and I have very little ambition in the trade, and yes, almost blind and dangerous. But I'm not going to just sit in a chair and wait for it to pass. Ignacio would have preferred me to sit and meditate, but there's nothing to think about now, I told him, snatching his cigarette by touch and taking a forbidden drag. I've already thought everything thinkable, I said, taking an even deeper drag. Thinking, I repeated, moving the butt out of reach when Ignacio tried to take it from my fingers—I accidentally hit the light bulb—I've been thinking since the first time I went, against my will, into an eye doctor's waiting room. Since then I've done nothing but think about the future, and how I'll never see it. Think about that twisted and recalcitrant doctor saying I was carrying a time bomb inside me, ticking faster and faster. He reported all the medical details to my mother, I went on, as if I wasn't sitting right there next to her and getting splashed by all the sticky, acidic saliva he was spouting. The doctor never looked at me, but the thick lenses of his eyeglasses are burned into my memory, and the clogged corneas criss-crossed with thin lines, those miserable, miniature eyes that from the doctor's very depths had foreseen this moment. Then I remembered, now without telling Ignacio, the way the doctor adjusted his black frames atop his nose while he murmured that maybe—but only maybe because no one can be sure—that maybe in a few years the diseased organ could be replaced with another, compatible one. And I remembered having thought about what it would be like to see through foreign eyes. The doctor's myopic eyes, I said aloud, raising my voice, his eyes made me more afraid than the future of my own, because they are eyes that have followed me and are still coming after me; even in dreams, Ignacio, those rabbit eyes. I don't have anything left to think about, I repeated. Think about it yourself, if you want. Really think about it, I insisted, raising my black eyes toward Ignacio and feeling I was losing my balance. I said it like a challenge, like an accusation, like a reproach, because it wasn't the first time I'd said this to him. I'd begun to say it six months before, starting with the dinner we gave Ignacio after his talk, the dinner I'd attended as a doctoral student, and where I'd sat down across from him to tell him I wrote, too. How I'd started in journalism but then they kicked me out for falsifying the objective truth of the facts, and I moved on to fiction, one hundred percent pure, I'd told him, caressing his leg with my calf. And to prove it I put my latest novel on the table, explaining that I'd condensed my name. So are you or aren't you Lina Meruane? Sometimes I am, I said, when my eyes let me; lately, I'm less and less her and I go back to Lucina. The extra syllable bled sometimes. Ignacio's face took on a puzzled expression and he chose not to believe my insinuation that I suffered from a defect that could leave me blind. Blind, I said, without dramatics, without losing my smile while we had a long drink while the distance between us got ever shorter. He should really think about it before he paid my bill and invited me into the taxi, I told him, before he touched me, gave me that wet kiss on the ear and then on the lips, before my sighs that were used but felt new, before my absolute silence, before he ever brought me a pancake breakfast in bed, or strummed that languid, cloying bolero on an old guitar, before he ever asked me to stay. To stay. First, yes, think about it. Think about it hard, I told him, looking at him fiercely, hoping he wouldn't think for too long, obliging him to at least pretend to think. Ignacio, I thought, now without insisting; Ignacio, open your eyes, you still have time.

price is right

There beneath the hair, inside his skull, in all those brains, Ignacio resolves that we should go out. Go out immediately, at a run if possible. We've spent the whole morning stuck inside waiting for the secretary's call, him wandering around the house, me very still, immersed in a nineteenth century novel that an unknown reader whispers to me from the walkman. Ignacio shakes me. I press pause, stop. The secretary just informed him that I can't have an appointment until Monday. What happened to Friday? No one canceled, no one is going to miss their appointment today, Ignacio says Yuku told him. Desperate and inconsolable, Ignacio announces that if we don't go out we will die of suffocation. We should go out and do something: look for furniture at second hand stores, for example. I wouldn't be able to choose anything by myself, you have to come, he insists, and I accept because never have I had more free time. Never as much as I do now, in the Manhattan streets full of deadly potholes and manholes with ladders that lead down to hell. The light hits my face but I can't touch it, I can't use it, and I walk through the city like I'm on a tight rope, leaning against Ignacio who walks at a different pace, syncopating his unmistakable steps with other, unfamiliar ones, sharp-heeled and rushed, that wound the pavement. We rummage among furniture made of smooth and wild wood that evoked exotic birds and mandrills, lichens, African songs; and there is also the scent of candied peanuts and caramel apples, of pretzels, bagels just out of the oven, grazing our noses. Nothing Ignacio sees convinces him, and I, who can't see enough and who follow his description of the world with only my fingertips, am afraid I'll fall over at any moment, struck down by heat and displeasure. Then we go into a new furniture store and we rest by trying out some armchairs under dry, conditioned air. Can I help you? says a voice equally cold and dry but more inclement, and I know Ignacio feels duty-bound to give explanations, improvising a British accent that comes out respectably well. He talks about how our house is bare, how we only have, for now, a mattress on the floor and a dozen unopened boxes and suitcases. And a couple of rugs, and a scratch on the floor, I correct him through clenched teeth, no talent for posturing. I suspect Ignacio is looking around, that on the inside he is furnishing the postcard from nowhere: coffee table, sofa, recliners, and chairs that would have to survive us like the children we'll never have. While he describes what our house will be like, I organize all that furniture we can't afford in an imaginary budget. And the light now is so tenuous. When the saleswoman turns around Ignacio decides in the blink of an eye that the purchase can

23

wait for a better moment. And he drags me out to the scorching street and I still hear him saying, breathless, more light, we have to have enough light, that's the most important thing, right? And yes, yes, sure, light, bulbs and lamps and screens, all that, I answer, breathless myself, already up to my neck with him in a store full of lamps. Lamps that are old but mended, like the store's owners: a sixty-something couple with long-lived lamps their own hands have refurbished. The younger man goes up the stairs to bring a lamp down. Are we only going to buy one? They're not cheap, answers Ignacio, and what do we want another one for? So we have enough light, I say. So we don't have a one-eyed living room, I add. Always two, just in case. We argue. The older one straightens his neck and decides for Ignacio that yes, it's always better to have two. *Lo está diciendo porque tiene un ojo en blanco*, Ignacio grumbles defensively in Spanish. A white eye? What happened to your eye? I ask, turning to the old man. I feel Ignacio squeezing my hand while he apologizes for me, explaining that I'm asking because I have a problem with my sight, too. A problem, I repeat, I'm practically blind. Ignacio lets go of my hand then and puts his own away in his pocket, along with his metro card. I wait. I had a stroke, the salesman says, a stroke right here in my eye, he adds. There was no way to revive it, he says. An eye isn't a heart. It's not even half a heart. It's much less, I add, that's why we have two. The old man stands there reflecting, but not about what I'd just said. His dead eye never really bothered him much, he explains sadly, though without really explaining himself. He clears his throat and says that his people were dying back then. In the eighties, I say, asking but really affirming, because suddenly I know what he's going to tell me. I know that he is, in his way, a survivor. That many people like him were filled with ganglia, with inexplicable ulcers, and that some went crazy or blind before sinking into stigma. That stigma had brushed against me and left a splinter behind: someone, maybe a decade ago, had told me that their AIDS diagnosis had been the closest thing he knew to having diabetes. That someone had identified with me, and then that someone had started to die in the eyes. The last time I saw him, he was blind. Only he and I are left, said the voice of the old man next to me, succinct as a summary trial. He was a judge of just causes, talking to himself. Only he and I, he repeats. I'd like to know where the other old man is; I'd like to be able to turn around, look toward the back of the store, where the old finger is surely pointing and expecting my eyes to follow. Losing this eye was the price I paid, he says without regret: the small price of staying alive.

a place in the north

Eight in the morning on a suffocating Monday. He's taking a shower after first preparing the syringe for me with clumsy fingers, and I inject myself with insulin before bathing. He makes his breakfast and my coffee with milk as I rummage among the black clothes in the closet, zip up my boots, adjust my glasses—also dark—and we head out like commandos on a secret mission: he's describing obstacles on the sidewalks and giving clues to the initiate, he's the militia leader who supplies street names for her to memorize, inserts the metro card into a slot before she can move through the turnstile. He is the one who instructs her on the number of steps leading to the platform, and he announces a long step to cross the gap. The doors of the car close and the trip begins. Are you nervous? But nervous isn't the word, not nervous or anxious or worried, not even overwhelmed. I feel like a pregnant woman awaiting her misfortune. And the trip toward my fate was long, but eventually the train stopped at the station and we were walking again along a thunderous route that threatened to leave us deaf as subway rats. But we arrived and we got off the train and went up stairs without holding the railing because who knows what fingers, what saliva and hair has slid over it and coated it in misery. We held hands as we walked. Swept along by the tumult of bodies that pushed us and stepped on the heels of our shoes, just that, the touch of our fingers, was the most intimate thing that could happen. Ignacio never stopped squeezing my hand to announce obstacles and to warn me of pedestrians who were running across on the yellow or even the red light. Now we had reached the real pretzel smell of Madison and 37th. A dog barked, standing still amid screeching brakes. The river soaked the air in low, frayed clouds that left the pigeons breathless. I went along asking for atmospheric pictures to fill in the holes in my imagination, and I asked questions that grated on Ignacio. Is the north still to my left? Yes, there it was, the north was where it always was, with its thick sky. I couldn't lose focus, my entire being demanded a multiplied concentration, an absolute dedication to the geography of things. And my head was buzzing, it was heating up with the images that every one of Ignacio's words stirred up in my memory. He said Central Park, and my head filled with blue ducks and tadpoles in phosphorescent lagoons defying the tourists.

He said Columbus Circle and I filled up with brides posing under a hollow and silvered planet with their future ex-husbands. He said step, careful, and I foresaw curbs much higher or much lower than they really were. Ignacio whispered we're on Lexington and then something different happened, I didn't see the street's idiosyncrasies anymore, but rather the sign of a hospital that was just a few blocks further north. I saw in my mind's eyes the room where I'd stayed for a long time; I saw the first black nurse of my childhood, the wide, toothy smile and the majestic air it gave her, I heard the hungry laughter that seemed to arise from deep inside her, but I couldn't remember her name. The nurse and all the children in that room were made of wax; they all had definite faces but no identities. I had lost mine there, too. I understood all of a sudden, alarmed, that it was there, north of a *gringo* doctor's office, where the long story of my blindness had begun.

sleepwalker

There were a lot of people waiting to be seen; we'd be spending an ungodly amount of time in that office painted with stripes and crumbling to pieces. There I was, standing next to Ignacio on the other side of the desk from Lekz's secretary, a disheveled Doris who wore a shirt as a dress over stockings. And flip-flops. Yes, whispered Ignacio later, she was wearing the same outrageous gold flip-flops, with pale and swollen toes peeking out, their nails a strident color. It was the same gray Doris I knew very well, a Doris who shouted into the phone as she argued with patients, who controlled the doctor's schedule with an unyielding hand.

I heard a listless greeting from afar, and I imagined her sprawled out as she slept during her commute from New Jersey, arriving at the office before Lekz with a box of donuts in hand. I also thought that even before Doris got there, Yuku would be in the doorway squinting her light eyes, an efficient Japanese assistant monitoring a frenetic eight on her wristwatch and wondering why Doris was taking so long, whether her train had stalled for good in the tunnel under the water. Yuku understood delayed trips, being suspended over the ground; she was never going to repeat that single, anguished trip of thousands of aerial kilometers, or rather miles, from Tokyo. I was still anchored to Ignacio, who was filling out my paperwork with the secretary. They were arguing, yelling, and I retreated from the noise, completely lost in the void of myself until Ignacio burst the bubble by poking his finger in my ribs. Lina! He pulled me toward him and nervously stammered another Lina in my ear: Doris is waiting for you. Who? Doris? Doris! I said, pursing my lips, confused, opening my eyes too wide, what is it? Though I only saw her in shadows, I could guess at her scowl. Without hearing her, I could reconstruct the question she'd just asked, calling me by my official name, the one on the forms. Did I or did I not still have the same medical insurance? Yes, of course, in my very best English, the same insurance. But what good had it done me to have it, I thought then without saying it, if it couldn't insure me against this. But yes, I said again, everything is the same, same university, same books growing old under a layer of dust, the same social security number, the same solitude now shared with Ignacio. Everything was the same, and yet it all seemed radically transformed. Doris considered the

28

interrogation over, and sent us to sit down. And might I know why you weren't answering the questions? I heard Ignacio say testily, cracking his knuckles. How am I going to explain things about you that I don't even know? Do you think I'm psychic? I can't tell what you're thinking, he concluded, tucking his shirt into his waistband to train hands that wanted to smoke but couldn't. But no, Ignacio, of course not, and it's a good thing too that you can't read my mind, I answered without thinking about what I was saying. And then I said to myself: I'll never let you see what's inside here, things I don't even tell myself. And then, finding my voice, I explained that I hadn't known to whom Doris was talking. I didn't see the gestures that went with her questions, nor could I read her lips or the wild movement of her hands. Being like this, in a fog, is like being asleep and awake at the same time. It's like being a little deaf. Ignacio nodded because he knew what it was to take off his glasses at night and be deaf. He rubbed his eyelids, or I imagined that he rubbed them, under his glasses. He sighed near my ear. Then he took my arm and didn't let go again.

overtime

It wasn't minutes but rather hours, days, months in that waiting room, with its constant crossing and uncrossing of legs, its dragging of shoes toward the bathroom and its plopping into dilapidated chairs. Ignacio dozed, his head lolling every now and then. A person had settled in to my right and was letting out aggressive sighs while turning the pages of a magazine surely full of depressing stories meant to raise your spirits. I heard yawning, the endless music of the minute hand, and finally an anxious standing up, approaching the secretary to ask for explanations for the doctor's delay. Doris took her nose out of her papers to remind us all with well-practiced coldness that one had to take time to consult this particular doctor, because this eye doctor only took serious cases of blindness. That is, said Doris, imitating the doctor's tone and clearing her throat like the spokeswoman of terror that she was, this doctor was only interested in extreme cases, eyes *in extremis*, the ones that required extraordinary acuity; Lekz, Doris went on, swallowing a cookie she was chewing with her mouth open, Doctor Lekz was interested in taking his time on every eye, in searching retinas for the sibylline presence of other illnesses of the body, AIDS, for example, syphilis, tuberculosis, and she went on listing them while she twisted a lock of hair with a finger. Badly-treated diabetes, high blood pressure, even lupus. Because the eye, her perverse, ire-filled tone went on, the retina was our life record, the mirror of our unfortunate acts, a perfectly polished surface that we spend our existences ruining. For all the damage we had caused, now we would have to wait our turn: wait without giving lip, or simply leave. No exceptions were made, because everything the doctor saw in that office was already exceptional. And it wasn't just a speech of Doris's. I had verified her words during uncountable hours waiting in that room, and also later on in the examining room. I never noticed Lekz rushing a single syllable or discreetly checking the time; there wasn't a single clock on the walls of his office, no phone ever rang, he didn't have a cell phone. No one ever interrupted him. He was an absolutely dedicated specialist, true Russian fanaticism inculcated by his Soviet lineage.

Each visit he went back over the patient's trajectory, asked for details, wrote everything down carefully in his record, although in an impenetrable script, and then, looking attentively into the eye, he seemed to light up. He was entranced before the pupil that his expert assistant spread before him after taking scrupulous sight measurements. It's Yuku, murmured Ignacio, as if reading my thoughts, here she comes with her eyedrops down the hall. She scraped her moccasins across the rug as she walked. She stopped in front of me and I straightened up, understanding what her doubly foreign tongue was asking me to do: tip my head back. Her fingers separated my eyelids and let fall, with precise Japanese marksmanship, two burning drops on my corneas.

let's see if it clears up

Lina, Lucina, Ignacio burst out, relieved or exhausted and confused, Lucina, getting tangled up among my names, Lina, with his back tight and his neck complaining: get up, Lekz is waiting for you. He had stationed himself by the door, Lekz, to let me enter while Ignacio stayed seated. He had me climb into the mechanical chair that I called electric and that he directed with his legs. He didn't need to tell me to lean my forehead against the bar and press forward. We'd had two uninterrupted years of training: he and I had practiced in that position like two resistance fighters, measuring our strength, taking our pulses and breaths; him examining me with his mechanical eye, me letting him scrutinize my inner workings. Letting him burn my retina with laser flashes, all so it wouldn't come to this. But now Lekz was taking his time sitting down across from me, he was bypassing the routine, eluding the exam, taking an interest in the detailed account of that night, the party, and the days that followed: what I had seen and what I could no longer distinguish. With his hand perhaps lost in his abundant hair, Lekz quizzed me about glimmers, flashes, iridescent sparks, and he wanted to know if I felt throbbing back there, behind the eye. He paused over my file before sitting down and finally lifting his arm to open my eyelid with his specialist fingers; only then did he peer into the dilated hole like it was a keyhole. What do you see, doctor? What are you seeing? I was asking a question and impatiently demanding an answer, a clearing of the throat, a sign he planned to give some kind of clue. But the doctor only let out perplexed sighs. He was seeing the same thing I was, I realized. The same bloody nothing I saw. In spite of his infinite magnifying lenses, Lekz couldn't make out a single detail on my retina. He leaned back absolutely resigned and said, We'll have to wait, see if it clears up so I can take a look at this mess. And if it doesn't ever clear up? I interrupted. If my body doesn't absorb its own blood? If it doesn't happen, he answered haltingly, if it doesn't ever happen—because, it's true, it's very unlikely an eye will clear up on its—if it doesn't disappear we'll have to take our chances and operate. Blindly. One eye, then the other. Lekz had bits of words between his teeth, pieces of little words hanging from his nose and sliding down his cheek, fragments of calamitous syllables that put off any immediate interruption. One eye and the other but not now, he said, later, dry as a recording, like a machine on repeat although Lekz's tongue seemed to be palpitating inside him. It was a throbbing tongue darting into my ear with its thick, still-warm drool.

Gulping air, choking down myself and all my frustration, my resentment, my blind hate for that life I wanted to tear away from, stifling myself so I wouldn't poison him with my rage, I told him with a thread of a voice to please take me out of that uncertainty and put me into the hospital. The operating room, immediately, tomorrow, please. I felt my eyes more swollen than ever, and throbbing. We have to wait, replied Lekz, immutable. Wait for what, doctor, a donor? But no. We are, he told me, still very far from a transplant. I was starting to slowly deflate, nicked by the scalpel of medicine. One whole month you have to wait, he insisted, making a note in my file. No fewer than thirty-one days, while your eyes clear up and we also clear up your case with the insurance company. I repeat, he repeated, implacable, before one month is up we cannot from any perspective operate on you. And in the meantime, doctor? What do I do in the meantime? Weren't you going to go to Chile to see your family? Go to Chile. Take a vacation.

pure Chile

It was too late to back out now: I would fly to Santiago on the date we'd agreed, and Ignacio would fly to Buenos Aires to give his speech. When he was finished, he promised, he would come to Chile to get me. The airline tickets, already printed and folded in the drawer, were our pledge to meet again. We had left the purchase of the Bolivian leg of our trip pending, but that flight had crashed and burned in the eye doctor's office. Boulivia, Lekz had said, making an effort to imitate my pronunciation, Boulivia, better we didn't go there, the high pressure and lack of oxygen would not only lead to altitude sickness, it could also burst my veins. But it hadn't been necessary to reach the heights of La Paz; all it took was a ninth floor with a view of the hollow left by the twin Manhattan towers. The red I saw, first in one eye, then the other, had settled the question of that trip. We would not go to Bolivia. And I wouldn't go to Argentina, either. Now I'd only fly to Santiago, I'd go without doubt, without hesitation, without delay: I was leaving in just a few days, and still. The phone calls from Chile started up, with a calling card or charges reversed, calls insisting that I travel sooner. That I should have the surgery there, where they were: my family, that turbulent clan of Mediterranean origins, armed to the teeth with love. Have it where they, all together or in shifts, could take care of things. Come with me to surgery, if necessary. Give instructions to the specialists. Advise me during my convalescence. Without realizing, they were conspiring against the little inner peace I had, against my powerful need to be a little alone with my fears and my enormous ingratitude. With myself and my dark purposes. But they were having none of that. They interrupted me. They held forth without listening to me. They promised prayer chains and homemade remedies without giving a thought to the agonizing state of my phone bill. They swore my anxiety would disappear under the weight of their own. Don't worry about a thing, they repeated in a chorus, a rowdy and tense chorus, not a thing, because added and multiplied and all tallied up, the balance of my family's anxiety would crush my own, which only went up and up, swelling like yeast and secreting a suffocating bile. Red lights were flashing everywhere: the word *care* stung, *loss of control* burned, *return* was dangerous and *have surgery in Chile* a punishment to which I didn't plan to subject myself. I had already agreed once before to see that other doctor, with his inflated cheeks, who diagnosed eyes from atop an imperious podium. You're about to burst, he'd told me, putting on determinist airs. I don't know how you aren't already completely blind, because any minute now. Here there is nothing to do except remove them, he finally said, looking at me fixedly and inflexibly, with impatience, letting me know that other patients were waiting. I would never go back. I'd promised myself. I'd told them that and yet, possessed of an atomic energy, they exhorted me to give him another chance. The no I gave them was round. An upper-case no. At the other end of the line they complained about my lack of willpower, my lack of consideration, my lack in general: my absence, my dispassion, my contempt for religion. They reproached me for their rushed and perhaps wrong but now old decision, at thirty years old—years that had been happy until then—to return to Chile when I. To suspend all their plans when I. And the phrase hung suspended, incrusted in all of their teeth. No one said: that disease, yours. No one said the tests, the diagnosis, the daily injections, the special diet, my mother's exhaustive care, and a life far from family support. They didn't talk about the difficult decision to leave splendid jobs in that hospital where overspending was the norm, nor of the fortune my parents would have amassed if only I. They didn't say it, but there were truths hanging by the thread of that pause. Truths swinging in the breeze. It was an insult that I'd returned to the same city three decades later, at the age my parents were when they'd left it. And I was paying for that affront with a new technical glitch in my anatomy. They insinuated that returning to

Chile to be with my parents was the right thing to do. They half-said it while the timer ran on my international bill and they finally said it while I visualized my body being sucked out into an abyss, my skeleton covered in its muscle and fat falling vertiginously toward Chile, my skin stretched ever tighter, my hair electrified, all my parts attracted by the law of national gravity, as I turned into an amorphous substance that, when it fell, would flatten the rest of my numerous family. I would crash into them, they would fall one after the other in a line across the tabletop. They'd knock one into the other, propelled by the weight of my mother, the stoutest of all our dominos and at the same time the most fragile.

blackmail

(Urgent for us to take a break. We'll be right back after this pause, as the movies during the dictatorship used to announce before kidnapping the steamy scenes that never returned. A long break and then we'll see, I thought in all my uneasiness. A period without seeing each other and without talking on the phone, so you can think. I was the one who decided on the break, wagering that the interruption would work like an evil love potion. That's what I thought, but who knows what you were thinking when you unhappily accepted that pact of silence. We were thinking separately, but simultaneously. We thought differently, but at times we thought the same thing. And you also had your friends thinking for you. How it was necessary to resolve that long-distance mess, that ethical dilemma, the emotional blackmail the blind woman was subjecting you to. They all thought about it in their own way.

Carmen corrected tests with one hand and used the other to stir and taste her *ají de gallina*, while her mouth complained about her son's villainous father. Osvaldo was planning a marriage celebration that we wouldn't be attending. Gaetán, training for his next ballet without focusing on the steps but laughing, nervous, shouting before the mirror. In his house, Julián smoked another cigarette slowly and gossiped through the keyboard with Carmen, who took a while to respond and copy Osvaldo, who would tell Gaetán, the other groom. Laura answered her emails preparing her summer classes, exhausted or maybe bored. Mariana put on lipstick, attending to her eyelashes that coiled like spiders; she smiled, pursed her mouth, making faces at herself in the mirror, choosing just the right one, the correct way to think about this matter. Piously? Perfidiously? And she talked to the mirror of your bad luck. Your bad eye. Of your becoming my seeing eye dog. That's what they said to each other but only Arcadio dared say it to you, in the cafe on the corner, without making a scene. No flailing or gesticulating, not even mussing his hair since he'd just shaved it all off. Biting into a waffle cookie thin as a host, dropping a pinch of sugar into his espresso and a drop of cream or maybe skim milk, pausing briefly, dazzled by the shine of his own skull. That woman, he said, with a calculated and dramatic pause, she isn't your girlfriend, she's a blackmail artist. And he took another sip of his coffee. When you heard that you lost it, you turned into another Ignacio, and the new Ignacio's eardrums flinched, his gums winced, his tongue dried out. He sat for a moment petrified with the cigarette hanging from his lips, afflicted by a sudden pain in the pit of his stomach. That Ignacio paid his part of the bill and took off, livid but most of all dizzy, secreting acid, overcome with disgust. His brain recoiled like a live oyster drenched in lemon juice. But in his own way, that pitiless way, that cold and offensive, son-of-a-bitch way of Arcadio's, he spoke something of the truth, something I had also seen in all my blindness. He's right, I told you after hearing you kick the door and then unscrew the lid from the antacid tablets. He's right, I repeated, consciously sowing resentment toward your friends. They all think it but they don't say it to you, or haven't you noticed the way they speak to you lately, or what they talk about when they call, how I don't exist in their conversations? And I went on struggling to separate my socks from the wool stockings designed to endure Chile's raw winter. Arcadio hasn't said anything you didn't already know, I added then to your stern silence, without for an instant stopping my folding, long- and short-sleeved shirts, my jacket. All black, literally black but also black like the hate I professed for all of them, especially Arcadio. That friend of yours, I insisted in all frankness, feeling you were filling up with gasses, that you almost weren't breathing, that Arcadio has hit the nail on the head. And then, kicking my half-empty suitcase you said, violent, the nail, that motherfucker, *me cago en Dios*.)

wheelchair

Time was speeding up. A shower. A brushing of teeth. A drying of the face. Full suitcases that exhale on closing. A Dominican taxi ordered by telephone and the subsequent arrival of a taxi that would be anything but yellow. The driver, who spoke a

Caribbean Spanish, barely said a word to us, turned up the radio and muzzled us with a merengue that could have been bachata. My head had already set off on its own trip, and only the shell of my body remained, disregarded in the backseat. We were starting to put mental miles and silence between us, although we were still tied with an invisible and elastic cord. I could barely make anything out through the fog, but what I saw in that moment in horror, in terror, with true consternation, was that I was about to lose everything Ignacio gave me. I would no longer have his arms to guide me, his legs to direct me, his voice to warn me. I wouldn't have his sight make up for the absence of my own. I would be left even more blind. I realized I had been clinging to Ignacio like ivy, wrapping him up and entangling him in my tentacles, suctioning him like a leech stubbornly stuck to its victim. That imminent flight was like a knife slicing between us as the taxi approached the airport, and my adrenaline started flowing. The cut was happening, it was turning into a deep wound, and the taxi left us at the terminal and Ignacio paid and took charge of my suitcase. The laceration was happening, had happened, in the security line as we moved forward in slow motion. Then, in fast forward. Ignacio took care of my passport check, he showed them my university student visa, the appropriate I-20, he asked them to give me an aisle seat, though in other times I would have chosen a window so I could watch the clouds during takeoff, and then he gave my luggage to the workers at the conveyor belt, took my hand and announced that the wheelchair had arrived. What wheelchair? I started to laugh, but, don't laugh, Ignacio told me, I'm serious about the chair. A chair? A *wheelchair*? Why did you ask for that? I have two legs! Ignacio put his arms around me while I fought him, elbows flapping, but he put his arms firmly around me and soon he was a straightjacket, one that smelled of ashtrays and old, acidic sweat, a straightjacket that not only squeezed me until I cracked, it covered me in kisses: my temple, my nose, my ear. The straightjacket talked into my ear in a barely audible voice, and convinced me it was better for an airport employee to take me through immigration and go with me to the gate. That way I wouldn't have to hold anyone's hand. Wheelchair, I grumbled, swallowing saliva and brushing a lock of hair roughly from my face. Lina, panted my straightjacket again, cutting off or squeezing my name, Lini, everything will be all right, I promise, don't cry, *por favor*, that makes me feel like shit. In the blink of an eye you'll have crossed the mountains and you'll be in Chile, Ignacio went on, as if that were any consolation. And I'll be there in a few days, he finished, finally loosening his arms. And then I nodded and sat down and plugged some excessive sunglasses onto my face, and the chair started sliding backwards, and his voice gradually dissolved in the crowd while I finally sobbed freely.

count to a hundred

Ignacio is still in the airport, a disconcerted frown on his face. Ignacio standing under the glowing screen. Departures. Arrivals. His glasses glint over his now-empty eyes. It's an aged and ruined Ignacio. An Ignacio cracked like an old statue on the verge of collapse. His shirt with the sleeves rolled up and his linen pants utterly tattered and his dull bronze shoes fixed to the floor. Centuries have passed, I think, and there he remains, covered by the ash or dust of my departure, clutching the anxious kiss I blew to him from a distance and enduring the unintelligible, cosmopolitan whisper of the travelers around him. His hands empty, he wished like never before for a cigarette between his fingers. I had vanished and already forgotten him, and I made my way among the travelers pushed by a woman with an iron will. She must have been obese, because she dragged her feet, she shuffled and complained. But she wouldn't give up for all that. With the canine bearing of every good civil servant, she would carry out her mission. She knew all the terminal's nooks and crannies, all the rules of the security checkpoint, every one of the employees. Her booming black voice cleared our way of any obstacles, and she pushed me up to the very door of the cabin. And with an offhand "There you are, ma'am," she dumped me there. I got up as though on a spring. Alone. Without asking the attendants for help, I felt my way along the backrests counting seat numbers until I reached my spot and could sink down. The passengers went on stowing their suitcases and briefcases and bags, jackets and coats and all kinds of colossal gadgets that barely fit in the overhead compartments. They talked about being overweight, they laughed, they excused themselves diplomatically for stepping on each other, Ay, sorry, thank you, *pucha que no entra esta huevada*; that's what their voices said as they melded into an incoherent tangle of words. I just had my backpack with the syringe ready to inject myself, and that's what I did: I took off the cap, stuck the needle in wherever it fell, and pressed the pump, ignoring the uncomfortable sighs around me. Then I fastened my seatbelt in the hopes of dying for at least a little while on that overnight. But I wasn't going to fall asleep, not yet, unfortunately. Because suddenly I noticed my legs were shaking, and that due to a strange but effective mechanical chain reaction, my whole body was trembling. My knees were clapping together like cymbals. My teeth were chattering. Wait a minute now, I said to myself. What's this? Am I having a seizure? But it wasn't a seizure, it was an electrical discharge that arose intermittently from my nerve center. This is just what I need, I thought, separating from myself and grabbing hold of Lucina, the Lucina who was me as I moved closer to Chile, and I grabbed her, like that, by the shoulders, and I started to shake her violently and to tell her, that is, tell myself: not now, Lucina, not a stupid panic attack, don't put on a little show now and make them kick us off the plane and leave us at the airport. Right now, I told her, telling myself, you're going to count to ten or a hundred, forwards or backwards, now, ok, get going, we're counting now. And that's what I did, but starting with *uno* and getting quickly to *seis* and when I got to *diez* I kept going without stopping because my disobedient body still wasn't under control: the shaking was worse. And so it went from *treinta y cinco* to *sesenta y siete* and when I got to a hundred I started again, but in English this time: three five six, and I remembered as if I were back there, that was how I used to count when I was seven years old in the school I went to when I returned to Chile. In New Jersey I'd forgotten all my Spanish. Later, in Santiago, I'd forgotten English. Now I'm forgetting myself, I thought. I took a breath, covered my nose, went into the numerical trance of that divided childhood, and that's how I reached a hundred again and started over, one more time, in one of my languages, thirty-three, *treinta y tres*, thirty-three.

claw

Count the next morning, too. Count instead of dropping pebbles that would guide my way back, or breadcrumbs that the birds would have eaten if I were crossing an enchanted forest and not walking down an airplane aisle. So I walked and counted seats, in search of the bathroom. Twenty-four. Everything under control, I told myself, balancing on the chemical toilet. On my way back the turbulence started, and my hand became a claw clutching awkwardly at the air, trying to grab hold of a backrest but landing, instead, on something warm, soft, meaty. My owl-fingers with their badly trimmed nails had come to rest on a shoulder. Or a breast. Or was it an ear? A sleeping body that I was shaking awake. I'm sorry, I stuttered, not really knowing where to direct my apology, I'm sorry, trying in vain or more like pretending I was trying to retract the claw from the mouth that opened suddenly to complain. What is this idiot doing? I heard a voice say, waking other people up. Trying not to fall over, I slid my hand up over a forehead of rough and impatient folds, and there my hand stayed, seizing up as we hit violent turbulence. Realizing the precarious balance I found myself in, my torso leaning forward, the woman took a firm hold of my hand, pulled it finger by finger from her face, and forced it back to where it belonged. That's your seat, she groused, as if I didn't understand anything, as if I were mentally challenged or worse, to her: a *gringa*. Take one step back, she said, and maybe talking to her companion she murmured, if she'd take those glasses off, maybe she could see something. That accent, so unmistakably Chilean, harbored the glacial poem of the mountain peaks and their snows in eternal mid-thaw, the dark whisper of the south dotted with giant rhubarbs, the mourning of roadside shrines, the herb-garden smell, the rough salts of the desert, the sulfurous copper shell of the mine open to the sky. The entire nation embodied in the bitter, uncertain tone of that traveler who suddenly, as I lifted my glasses, understood. Blind? There was no need to explain to her I wasn't entirely blind, that I could distinguish contrasts. That I knew the flight attendant had opened a window and it encased me in its rectangle of light, and that someone else had closed it again, that the light beams of a movie were shining intermittently. I was a blind woman capable of detecting flashes of light, and, from afar, also the compassion of others that came after surprise. Blind? That compassion made me crawl with hate. Blind! she said again. Sit down, please, repeated the woman, but I couldn't move. That pity of hers had paralyzed me. It had me stuck there while my memory traveled quickly into the past. The woman must have thought I didn't understand, and as if I were a dog trained in British English, she raised her voice and said sit, miss, you're going to fall, sit! Shit, I thought, but instead of cursing her I chewed a short *sí* and another s*í, ya le oí*, I heard you, ma'am, and I even understood. I speak the same Spanish as you. I turned around and sat down diligently, turning on my walkman to listen to a book, any book, and I buckled my seat belt and tightened it to the point of asphyxiation.

connections

Sunk once again in another wheelchair, I wanted to be a ghost stealthily returning to settle old scores, to cross through the world without feeling it instead of bumping awkwardly into it all. But as it was, rolling through the tube of the airport, the specter I hoped to be realized, overwhelmed and amazed, that I had materialized again. I'd been recognized. Someone was bawling the *Lucina* that the calendar of saints records only as an etymological error, like Lucila or Lucita or Lucía, or even Luz, which is so close to Luzbel, the demon of light. Under the hallucinogenic effects of anesthesia, my mother—who until then had professed nothing beyond the doctrines of pediatrics—thought she heard the child I was starting to be babble a name. Lucina! my mother called out when she heard me cry between her legs, and in ecstasy she repeated it to be sure. Lucina. The delirium was getting to me too, since that was the very word I thought I was hearing there in the passageway. Lucina. It grew in decibels. Lucina! Anticipating the body that emitted it like a lightning bolt that comes seconds ahead of the thunder. It was following me at full speed. Lucina? it said, doubting, ever closer, with an inquisitive nasal inflection, opening its way through the people. I heard panting breath and then a spasmodic what...? happened to you...? And without waiting for the answer I didn't plan to give, the same thing again, more formally this time: what happened to you, Lucina?, still agitated from the run. Why are you in a wheelchair? Did you break your leg? I would have liked to leap with all my wheels and handles into the future, or jump into the past as off a cliff; but no, I take it back, I thought ipso facto, not into the past. The bearer of that voice could only come from a preterite tense to which I didn't want to return. There was no escape. The employee in charge of pushing me stopped so the excruciating interrogation could continue. I pricked up my ears but could not place the voice anywhere in the fog of my adolescence. Without asking, so as not to give myself away, I followed what he was saying in search of clues. He almost hadn't recognized me in those black glasses. They look straight out of DINA, he said, and then corrected himself. Are you going incognito? More like blind alter ego, I said to myself, praying he would leave. And as if sensing the impatience that was growing weedlike inside me, he corrected himself again. But they look great on you, are they from New York? From China, I murmured to myself, made in China or Taiwan or someplace in India. Imported direct from the street. (You gave them to me, Ignacio, and now you're wearing a pair just like them.) We were silent. The employee got the chair moving again but my interrogator refused to give up on the scene of our failed reencounter. He followed, filling the pauses, saying aloud that New York was a fan-tas-tic city, that the things happening there were in-cre-di-ble, ab-so-lute-ly crazy, how could people so immeasurably rich live on the same island with the kind of beggars you didn't even see in Chile anymore? He'd gotten on the subway with a troupe of hobos who had surely hopped the turnstiles, and later he realized that they slept in the cars or on the platforms or among rats so obese they looked like nutria. I heard him asking me if I hadn't heard of unbridled capitalism, the bankruptcy of the state, the successive closing of shelters. I didn't say anything, because he was already talking about the reason for his trip. September 11th. The first anniversary. A special report.

If only I'd known you were there, he said—because you were there, right?—because no one had wanted to talk to him, no one, not until he'd pulled at some threads and finally tracked some people down. You can't even imagine, he said, cutting himself off. And then he placed between us the word success. I imagined a swollen reporter drowning in emotion while he said. I found overlooked people, illegal immigrants, some of them Chilean! Dis-a-ppeared, he said, and I thought about that worn-out word while wishing for a moment to disappear myself. We were going down an escalator and he was behind me saying, no one has shown this yet, and I'm going to do it, my team and I, though it'll be my name on it. His name. Who could he be? I thought. And though I didn't really care, my left hemisphere was running through the archives of old names and forgotten faces, while the right, just as vehe-ment, was wondering shamelessly, if this was the guy who back in his day had sold us on the glories of a harmonious transition. I had masturbated his *success* in the backseat of a Citroneta before disappearing without explanations, leaving my name behind. And when does your report air? I asked just to say something, without realizing that the only possible date was September 11th. In two months. The people, he exclaimed, will know the truth! And the employee, who had sped up the chair's pace, braked all of a sudden and launched me forward. What truth, if I might ask? he asked defiantly, as if he were reading my thoughts but pronouncing my question in a Peruvian accent. The connections between our September 11th and theirs! What don't you understand? And the reporter addressed me once again, as if demanding professional complicity from me as an ex-journalist, to crown the conversation:

doesn't it strike you as an amazing coincidence, 9/11? It's not a coincidence and it's not repetition, I told him, annoyed. It's nothing but a strange double image.

rescue operation

My father comes to the rescue and pulls me out of my introspection. It's his bony tourniquet hand that falls onto my shoulder. His debilitated skeleton, his long femur I hold on to. He leans over to kiss my forehead and I extend my fingers to run them over his face, trying to trace his face into my palm. I touch him like the professional blind woman I'm becoming. My father is alive, I think, he's alive in there, inside his body. Then his voice, the word daughter, winds its way through the crush of passengers waiting for suitcases, and in my ear drum his relieved words echo: I had to insist before they'd let me come in and look for you. I imagine he gives a tip to the employee so he'll disappear, and then he says, as though bewildered, together again, Lucina, daughter. He says it in a voice of hope and sorrow, and I know that the hopeful tone is for daughter and the sorrow is for Lucina. No one but my father uses his saliva to glue those two words together into a single compound word: Lucina-daughter. That *daughter* is adhered to me, stuck like a throbbing shadow on my back. That *daughter* and I are for him the same person with a single dilemma. He must be observing us very seriously, trying not to feel anything, my father, pretending to be a tin man. If you probed him you'd hear his words echoing against the walls of his body. But my father's core is not totally empty. At the level of his eyebrows and just behind his eyes there

48

are machines of all kinds: a magnificent motor that propels him, slowly, forward; an extremely punctual clock, a colossal memory fit for details both indispensable and useless. There is also a punished heart in a dark corner that no one notices, except maybe, in secret, my mother. But among all these mechanisms lurks the risk of a malfunction. If the tension rises. If some sharp emotion. Danger sign, and then. Right now I'm afraid to think my father's silence could be a short circuit. An interruption in speech called going mute, cut-off concentration that could keep us from reaching his house. It's no secret that my father gets through difficult situations using distraction. He gets into his old Dodge like a crew member boarding a spaceship, and in that trance he holds long conversations with himself, or gives lessons in internal medicine, or delivers speeches, and he argues, discusses, gesticulates, until he finds himself in the parking lot of the hospital where he still works. He's on time but he doesn't know how he did it, which streets he took, which red lights stopped him. He could have run over a cat and not realized. But he gets out of the car and his true function begins: a doctor infallible in matters of the heart. Of organically rickety hearts. Hearts in need of pacemakers. Clogged carotids. Blocked arteries. And because my father is exclusively dedicated to non-amorous cardiac catastrophes, he doesn't know anything about ailing retinas. I know he'll ask for my test results out of habit; still sitting in my wheelchair, I prepare myself to tell him I didn't bring them. I didn't bring anything, Dad, I tell him. None of them? he asks, and I say no, not the angiography or the optical tomography or the fundus of the eye. I left hundreds of brutal images behind. I left the perimetry behind because it was depressing.

I didn't ask for copies of any reports. It wouldn't do any good for you to have them, I tell him, shutting down the conversation. My father stands possibly thoughtful and then he murmurs an I see, Luci, *hija*, dear, which is almost a rebuke. I've never wanted you to be my doctor, it's enough for you to be my father. The silence after that is so weighty that it seems to creak; my father dispels it by saying. It wasn't so I could look at them. I wouldn't understand, he confirms in a mournful tone. Because eyes today are not what they used to be. He falls silent again and glances, I'm sure, at the conveyer belt, motionless and still empty of suitcases. Then he says to me, although really he says it to himself because his murmur is almost inaudible: half a century ago eyes were different. We looked at them with naked eyes and we saw so little. The medicine I studied is outdated, he explains, and it's true. It was all left behind at the side of a rocky road with twisted, rusted-out signs blowing in the wind. My father is a species going extinct. All he can do is come to the baggage claim and find my suitcase for me. The belt starts to move, regurgitating shapes of different sizes, and my father asks me what color my suitcase is with that serenity so like him. Blue, I say, with wheels. That's all and it's enough. Here it is. Now let's get going.

old pajamas

(This is the father I would introduce to you when you arrived, Ignacio. A man crowned by frizzy salt-and-pepper hair that had always been thick but was now becoming sparse. The breeze lifted and mussed it and left him looking like a mad or sad scientist, tall but bent by the weight of the successive deaths life had obliged him to attend. My father now went ruminating along, dragging my suitcase and taking his usual long strides impossible to match, not noticing I was limping and clutching his arm. I had aged without warning, I'd filled up with aches and pains; the neurotic stiffness in my hip had gotten worse on the flight. Every movement set off a tense spark in my groin. I can't walk that fast, Dad, wait a second, I told him. Almost there, he replied, a little out of it, not noticing my difficulty, engrossed as he was in calculating the distance: no more than a hundred and twenty-four meters and a few centimeters to the airport entrance, then fifteen to the parking lot gate, he announced with military precision, while I went on shuffling like a penguin over the cold winter pavement. I unhooked myself from his arm and told him to go ahead. I can't. My father slowed his stride and took advantage of my exaggerated slowness to bring up the medical issue again. *Hija*, he said softly, for once renouncing his authoritarian instinct, wouldn't it be better for you to have the operation in Chile? I bit my lips, Ignacio, I bit them to keep from saying that I hadn't come to ask for more medical opinions, I'd made the pilgrimage to enough doctors' offices and no one had given me anything but anxiety. No, I'd come to say that I needed them, and that I never wanted to need them again. Dad, I murmured, we've had this conversation too many times. I was exhausted, and I knew my father was taking advantage of my weariness. I decided to let myself be carried along for a while on his deliberate, faltering but precise scientific disquisition. My father was the only person who could make me waver, but I'd learned to wear armor.

Trying to elude his reasoning, my mind drifted toward my father's least reasonable aspects, his most arguable and nostalgic facets, the most incoherent, the most inexplicable traits in a doctor of his ilk. My father in loose, worn-out pajamas, translucent from wear, in which he'd walk around the house like a nudist. My father in love with those pajamas, brought from New Jersey over thirty years before, and which he refuses to throw out in spite of my mother's pleas and her offers of better, softer, and especially more appropriate pajamas. Decent ones, says my mother, who even offers, instead of throwing them out, to cut them up, recycle them as rags so that my father's now very dead cells would pick up the house's grime and be of some use. I thought of my father half-naked and half-dressed, my exhibitionist father, my father; yes, I was looking for arguments to counter his accusations that I was an unreasonable, inconsiderate daughter, stubborn like my mother. The pajamas showed his own stubbornness, his disregard toward the shame and modesty of others. The neighbors who spied through the fence. Olga, who had lost all curiosity. You yourself, when you came, would avert your eyes from him. But my dear, answered my father, his voice rising in surprise, what do my pajamas have to do with all this? It's not the same thing to cling to pajamas as to a doctor, he added, surely blushing. Exactly, Dad, a doctor is much more crucial than a little piece of cloth. I only trust this doctor, you should understand that. And there the conversation ended. We went on walking slowly, both quiet, each chewing over our own thoughts, and suddenly I felt or I realized, Ignacio, that we had spent a long time wandering around in search of his old Dodge. Dad, I said, yielding to the role of daughter for a while. Is it far?

We're almost there, he replied, surely lying. My father had not bothered to look for the car; he'd forgotten why we were there. We were lost amid thousands of cars, but the air pushed us gently. The locks jumped up. The motor turned over. The mountains, I asked, are they snowy today? Snowy, no, it's snowing, he told me dryly. But you can't see anything, he added, the air is too dirty. The sky in Santiago isn't what it used to be, my father said wistfully. I opened the window like someone opening an eyelid, and I had the impression I was seeing the mountains snowy all the way to their bases, shining blindly in my memory. And I put my head out the window to inhale the breeze full of toxic particles that reminded me I was home. I let the grime penetrate my lungs, hearing, in the distance, the barking of invisible mutts.)

iron hand

She threw herself on my neck. A medusa, a jellyfish, an ocean flagellum, a gelatinous organism with tentacles that would cause a rash. There was no pulling my mother off of me. Her body contracted as if she were sobbing and she gave off a substance one hundred percent lethal. That poisoning by maternal venom would have brought on a dizzy spell, would have made me fall over in a faint. But no, there were no fainting fits or swoons. No ether or hysterical outbursts. Just a little ink to give some contrast to an opaque scene: my mother waiting for me atop her high-heeled shoes in the doorway, tapping her heels on the pebbles. She'd gotten up at dawn, worked erratically during the very first hours of the morning so later on she could leave the last acute patients to a troop of aspiring pediatric internists. And carrying the smell of the hospital, the smell of children vomiting the pus of their lungs all over her, my mother had returned home. Running red lights. Cruising over crosswalks and speed bumps without slowing down. And now she was outside, clutching the gate, letting the rain drench her. It would have been a perfect reencounter with rain falling on us. Falling in buckets. Pouring down. Driving us into the ground. But had it been raining I would have remembered the drumming sound on the Dodge's roof, I'd remember a downpour just like I remember the cutting cold of that winter. It wasn't raining, wasn't drizzling, there wasn't even a miserable, murderous hail falling. Only the snow clouds emptying over the peaks of some faraway mountains. Only a wind peeling the trees, ruffling the leaves and swirling them in eddies. Fighting that gust of impertinent air, my mother would be tending her hair, fresh from the hairdresser's hands; she'd be fluffing her mane upwards while her husband, whom she'd insisted on calling her "old man" ever since they were young, parked the car on the gravel. And maybe my mother was still smoothing a lock stiff with hairspray, nodding slightly at her own thoughts. Maybe she adjusted her glasses on her nose, maybe she stuck the tip of a painted nail in her mouth when she saw me get out of the car like a bride in black. A bride in mourning on my father's arm. In another invented memory, some fingers appear and energetically separate me from the old man, my mother's old man, though now she too is almost elderly. It's her arm, her hand, and my mother's invincible muscles that want to guide me, no limping or slipping, toward the door; she wants to save me from treacherous stairs, guide me across thresholds that lead nowhere, protect me from banging into book-cases. From obstacles crouching in corners. From the TV antenna that could pierce my eyes. The burner on the stove, the boil of the pots, the roar of the kettle. My mother tugs me along because the entire house is armed against me. She squeezes me with an iron fist, sticking her nails in through my sweater until she buries them in my flesh. Scratches. Deep cuts. Wounds that don't scar over: I'm gushing blood. I plead for help, but from whom? My older brother is meeting with some Mexican or maybe Colom-bian clients and he can't come to the phone. He sends a message through his secretary, who must be a sublime girl in high heels and a low-cut blouse, but who could just as well be a stuffy old lady with the voice of a young woman. Whichever it is, she tells me that *señor* Joaquín will call as soon as he's free. Tell him I'm in Santiago being devoured by a delicate carnivorous flower. But the woman hangs up before I say anything. Through the phone I only hear the continuous, irritating sound of a machine that records, monotonous, my cardiac arrest as it's happening. Better this way, I think. My big brother has his own issues, his own humor, biting, too black to hear my call for help. I turn, then, to my younger brother, another aloof wunderkind who in two curt words lets me know he's on his way, that he's almost here, that he's here. He honks his horn before coming in and sitting down to lunch. A sticky kiss falls on my cheek. Hey, sis, he says in English, casually. An old habit picked up in New Jersey. How was the flight, sis, could you sleep at all? He sits down at the table, stuffs a piece of bread in his mouth, and, still chewing, mutters a mom, you could let up just a little, couldn't you? Luci can't eat when she's in shackles.

I can call to mind those enormous black eyes of my brother's, his deep voice and his coal-black eyes. My mother, who forgot about smiling months ago, lets out a maniacal peal of laughter and lets go of me. My father, not realizing what is happening or maybe acting the crazy a bit himself, lets his big hand fall on top of mine and handcuffs me with his fingers. And my brother, chewing something that from its crunch must be a carrot or celery stick, says, slowly, but you're not totally blind, or are you? I hear gasps around the tablecloth and the strident music of a fork falling onto a plate, then Olga's discreet entrance with another dish and her immediate exit backstage, not daring to interrupt and say hello to me. And unaware a brawl is about to break out full swing, my brother Félix asks, completely calm—his amputated nerves are inherited from my father—another forbidden question. Where am I going to have the operation, in the end? What do you mean where? I ask him, raising my voice but holding back. There's never been any doubt about where. We'll talk about this later, my mother intercedes, giving me a kick under the table that was meant for someone else. There's nothing to discuss, I start to tell them, pushing away the plate of oily spaghetti that in any case I couldn't bring myself to eat, and knocking over a glass of red wine. I'm not going to see that doctor, I tell them, sensing a flurry of napkins falling over the table. Don't you remember what happened the last time I went? Hands mop up the wine; Olga reappears, lifting up my plate and wiping underneath it. And I manage to catch her and I ask her to sit down, because she is part of our life though my parents refuse to accept it, because I need her as my ally, because even if she's against me she should be part of this conversation and not turning a deaf ear behind the door. I'm not going to see him, much less be operated on by that specialist who looks down on all his patients, I don't care if he's Harvard-trained or a disciple of Barraquer. My post-Soviet doctor is better, he takes the time to explain my eyes to me and he doesn't jump to the knife like that aggressive Chilean eminence with a diploma that's *gringo* anyway. Someone picks up my glass, but it isn't Olga. Someone lets out a sigh of frustration, and I suspect it is my mother. Cancel the appointment, I insist. Because I won't go, not even if you tie me up. Not even drugged. You all hear me? Not even dead.

holes

If you're not exhausted, said Félix as he came tiptoeing into my room, if you're not absolutely worn out, come take a drive with me. Downtown, he said. I have a new project I want to show you. Show me? Tell you about, he replied, editing himself, adding, let's go for a ride! You feel like it? Do I feel like it? I yanked off my headphones, leaving half-finished the chapter of another novel I'd already read. I turned off the device and threw it onto the bed. I would have headed out into the street and crossed through blaring horns without looking, I would have forced the locks to get into any random car, I would have pressed my own foot to the accelerator just to get out of that house. I needed fresh air, even if Santiago's was radioactive. Now we can talk about the important things, said my brother as he fastened his seatbelt and constrained my body with the passenger side belt. As the car set off and began to gather speed, I looked into the rearview mirror with my mind's eye, the eye that later conceives memories. Félix checked behind him; my eyes were staring blankly forward. Right away Félix began talking to me about the tower he was involved in, involved up to his eyebrows, he said, with his team. But why build more towers? I thought. Towers are monuments in decline, you only have to build them and someone comes and knocks them down. But my brother unspooled his soliloquy with the modular details of the design, the widths and lengths of each floor, every one of the windows; he threw out names of materials, angles of incline, resistance calculations. He talked, absorbed in the downtown's architectural renovation, the urgent need to make room for the new, the empty lot's biography. I listened to him silently, thinking how at that insipid afternoon hour we would be surrounded by full buses, full taxis, maybe an empty cart coming from the central market, how we'd be traveling with an escort of shining and insolent cars destined to leave us behind. I thought about and almost saw the muddy and hostile river that Ignacio would come to feel was his, as with everything, as with too much. I struggled to listen to what my brother was saying, so young and euphoric, so indifferent. I let loose pieces of the city sprinkle over the map in my visual memory, Santiago's dirty avenues and the contours of its corners, handwritten signs with grammatical mistakes, shops selling used American clothes, the dubious cafes *con piernas* in the city center, certain streets that every Chilean knows and that I was going to introduce Ignacio to later, broken phone booths, carts selling cups of cold *mote con huesillo*. To your left is Plaza Italia (and the plaza appeared to me, Ignacio, the one that's now recorded by your eyes, the plaza with its Icarus carrying an excessive bronze torch), and to the right, he said, the refurbished, or rather, converted ex-Normandie, (the cinema where I watched midnight screenings of devastating Russian films, killing myself with cold, dying of fatigue), and here, Félix's voice interrupted my memories, here is Santa Lucia hill and its mural of the founding of Santiago (each word a spadeful of color in my head), you know where we are? I simply nodded before the panoramic format of my Santiago past as it went through my head. The car shot through the city like a meteor until we reached La Moneda palace, which appeared to me white, immaculate, the way it was before military helicopters flying overhead dropped bombs on it, and in the midst of the imagined offensive, with the soundtrack of the dictator's voice announcing his ignominious victory in the background, the live, guttural, articulate voice of my brother Félix slipped in, chronicling the square meters his tower would have, his invisible team's tower, once it was complete. Félix, I said, interrupting him: where are the holes? In La Moneda? What are you talking about, he answered impatiently. They rebuilt it ages ago! But I was talking about the buildings across Alameda, on Paseo Bulnes, the old buildings with walls colored by time and dust, perforated especially on the highest floors by devastating bazooka fire. Oh, yes, he said, those are still there, the gaping holes, and also in the less visible buildings on nearby streets you can see the holes from the machine guns fired by sharpshooters posted on neighboring roofs. Why do you ask? I'm not sure, I heard myself answer. And I also told him that I was thinking about the shards of the coup, so many acid shards eating away at the concrete. And I also thought, but didn't say, that those walls had witnessed everything, but were now blindfolded by a thick layer of soot that only fell away, a little every few years, in the earthquakes.

suicide techniques

We're on our way back. Between one stoplight and another my brother is compelled to ask for clinical details about my eyes. The technicalities of the surgery. The quality control of the instruments. The documentation required by the insurance company before they'll authorize surgery. He asked what options the doctors were considering: the outlook or the prognosis, that word that sounds more like an incurable disease than a remedy. And what are you going to do? asks my brother. If…without daring to finish the sentence. If things don't go well? I ask, not daring to be more precise. No one has ventured a hypothesis. I've suspended the future while I squeeze, thirstily, all I can from the present. But what are you going to do? insists my brother, if the thing doesn't go well? The Thing is the operation and it won't be one but two. I have two chances, I say. And if both operations fail? I pretend to reflect for a moment but I'm blank, and in that cloud appears an answer that I'd never considered. Kill myself? Another cloud now, a cloud of silence. My brother's face must be annoyed; his dim eyes blink in slow motion, while mine have forgotten to. I can tell from his measured but sarcastic voice that he doesn't think I could do it. And how would you do it, do *that*, in your condition? You wouldn't have anyone to lend you a hand, or at least an eye. My brother's words stick into me like safety pins, they wake me up. Lend me an eye, I say to myself, treasuring the image all I can.

Silence. You're very quiet, says Félix, aren't you? Yeah? I say, leaving a lot of air between his question and mine. Yes, very quiet. You haven't told me how you're supposedly going to do it, do *that*, he says, and he emphasizes the word so much I can see it in cursive, crushed by irony. How am I going to do it? I wonder secretly while I rewind suicidal tape in my memory. I press play on the paradoxical suicides. The lyrics of the song explain: what makes you live can kill you in excess. The refrain repeats: too much sun, too much sugar, too much water, too much oxygen. Too much maternal love. Too much truth. What are you talking about? interrupts Félix, who isn't one for subtleties while he's driving. I was remembering a friend who in the deep depression of a stampeding manic phase called me to ask for insulin. Twice I've gotten that call, from two different girlfriends, I tell him. And what did you do? asked my brother, wondering why those things never happened to him, confessing that he wouldn't know what to do. And he stops. What else could I do but send them to the pharmacy to buy their own poison? I say. To the pharmacy? In Chilean pharmacies, I say, they sell insulin without a prescription. You didn't know? Then it's my brother who sinks into a long silence, from which he emerges minutes later with aplomb, with self-possession, putting his hand on mine before he takes it away again to shift gears and assure me that I'm not going to do *that*. Commit suicide. He's right but I don't tell him so; nor do I clarify that neither of my friends went ahead with the insulin. My brother doesn't ask the question I expect, and I wonder why but don't have an answer. Fleeing the morbidity, employing his emergency humor, Félix says instead. I can only accept *that* in extreme cases. But Félix, since when do you defend assisted suicide? I ask, holding back an admiring smile. I start reminding him of angry arguments with my parents, because death, in our family, has always been dinner-table topic. We've attended medical classes in every after-dinner conversation. You're right, I wasn't serious, my brother says now, annoyed; just ignore me. Oh, but Félix, I think aloud, regretting that I can't see his face, regretting above all that I can't caress his eyelids, feel his eyes with my fingertips, Félix, I murmur, lightening things, I don't have any plans to do it, but you could really work things in your favor. Maybe there's an inheritance, and without me there'd be more for you two. It's so easy for a blind woman to fall from a balcony. So quick, such a sure ending. It's not a bad idea, says Félix, taking a sharp turn and speeding up; still, he objects, there's one problem we haven't considered. Who would take care of the cleanup? He honks the horn and brakes at a light and waits for a moment, he explains, for the light to change and me to answer. It's a somewhat peculiar worry, I tell him in a stagey voice. But fundamental, he says, without dropping his new character, and then he doesn't say anything more about that and instead opens his mouth to announce that we're there, and I hear a suddenly sad or mournful tone, I feel an awkward kiss between my eyebrows. You need help, sis? he murmurs, his voice as though strumming a chord in the air. No, I say, I'm good. And he tells me, too late, be careful not to bump your head.

the unconditional

(If I don't mention my older brother, it's because I never saw him.

I didn't see anyone well through the fog in my eyes, but I only heard from Joaquín secondhand: messages sent with a secretary, a call while he sped home to pack and say goodbye to his wife, who also complained of his absence, and his kids one after the other, almost clones, and his two maids. He'd rush out and arrive just in time to catch the plane taking off for China. He never managed to come by and say hi. I'm sorry, he told me, I'm dying to see you. Yes, don't worry, I answered, furious and resentful, offended as a mistreated lover. Have a nice trip, I told him, knowing in my whole body, from hair to feet, that he was running away from me again. I decided to let him go, forget him so much that I never even mentioned you to my brother: a good boy with bad luck, a good guy with a much better eye than you, Ignacio. Was it that I forgot him, or that it was better for you to know nothing about him? About how he started to run away from me when we were children, the day I came home from the hospital and fell on him like dead weight? Because the never-written contract of being an older brother made him into my slave. He took my hand and dragged me through the too-eternal snows of New Jersey, both of us wrapped in radiant orange raincoats with synthetic fur around the hoods; he would guide me like an eskimo to the bus stop, help me onto the yellow bus that picked us up every day, hand me the book I was reading so I'd be entertained during the ride; he carried my lunchbox and made sure I ate my food and sometimes his before he examined the leftovers. My brother was never more scrawny than in those photos, never more silent, more insomniac, more possessed and cornered. How old were we? Nine and seven? Eight and six? Ten and eight? Any and all ages, and in the background a bridge lit up to offset the winter afternoons. From the windows he surveyed the burning lights while I read some book from the school library and my mother cooked dinner. Joaquín went on observing the steel bridge, counting every one of its light bulbs while his body stretched and swelled, emerging from viscous childhood as from an egg. And he sat there one night with the bridge as his ally, finishing his homework, though really he was waiting for my mother to finish washing the dishes so he could tell her, his adolescent voice breaking, that studying and working at the same time was too much. Working? said my mother, looking at my father who was looking, cowed, at Joaquín. He was handing in his resignation and they accepted it because they weren't brave enough to make him be my nurse and my school tutor in addition to having to be my brother, which he hadn't even agreed to. No one had ever consulted him. He only wanted to study, he explained, his head sinking down between the blue lapels of his jacket, strangled by the striped tie, with pride and shame, frightened of himself. In exchange he promised to be the best in his class, restore their pride as parents. And then my mother lowered her head and said yes in a frightened voice; she was afraid of my brother, so circumspect, so gaunt, so forged of scrawny dignity, and my father gave him two little pats on the back to tell him sure, son, of course, of course, you could have said something sooner. And then I was left alone with them, at their mercy, terrified of the vigilance they called care, suffocated by the weight of improvised sins entirely of their making. I was left without the shield of my older brother. Félix, when he was born so much later—such a vulnerable tadpole—could never give me the same protection. Gradually I became a good girl at school and a spoiled brat at home, spending my time locked in my room with a pile of books. Joaquín disappeared into his math exercises, the three set squares, the circular ruler, the compass, alone; downcast and resentful, my brother walked through the halls at school solving equations and not noticing me, moving deeper into hard sciences, more and more like my father but afraid of girls because they all seemed too much like me, they all wanted something from him. So you'll understand why I haven't told you about my brother abandoning me and my parents abandoning him and later how I also abandoned them all, everyone, in search of someone with a true vocation for sacrifice, someone drowning in love or indoctrinated in the need to love, someone with an absurdly heroic passion, some guy with a pure and absolutely unconditional death wish.)

miles away

The irritating sound of the phone rang out at all hours in that house of doctors and patients. It rang during the day like nighttime alarms; it rang because my mother wasn't there, or because she was, but was taking a nap before leaving again to attend patients at her private practice, and in any case the phone could just go on ringing because my mother was a little deaf in one ear and Olga, completely. I pressed headphones over my ears, trying to focus on another drama about a suicidal heroine that went on turning uselessly in the cassette player while I debated whether to move on to the next novel. It rang and rang, but answering always entailed a risk. The risk that at the other end was a patient pleading desperately for help without stopping to wonder who he was asking. My father's patients were old men, decrepit but still strong enough to insist on spelling out their newest symptoms for me, the list of medicines prescribed, tests and their results, clinical histories. They were slavering old folks, they wouldn't stand for interruptions, they wielded their ellipses with sly intelligence. They weren't familiar with the full stop. What did they care that the doctor wasn't there, that I wasn't a secretary but only a daughter— a reluctant one, at that—and this wasn't the office but rather his private home? What they wanted was to smear someone with their dread of the imminent death creeping up on their heels. Other times through the receiver I heard the voices of the mothers of my mother's patients, and these also refused to stop and listen to my explanations, and insisted on asking, their hearts shattered or deeply grooved—asking themselves more than anyone else—what to do, my god what do I do, my daughter swallowed a bottle of pills, the snails in the garden, the potato peelings, she's ingested the paraffin from the heater in large, suicidal swallows. And then it was my turn to ask them questions: what were they doing on the phone with me and not in the emergency room? Hang up and run to the stomach pump. Not only was the telephone my parents', the calls were also for them. Only every once in a while did it ring for me, first the voice from a call shop establishing the connection, then Ignacio's voice from Buenos Aires, then my voice saying but no, no, you're breaking our agreement, didn't we say we weren't going to talk? Don't call me again. And then we would be quiet but we wouldn't hang up, Ignacio and I, punished by a strictly voluntary agreement. You're right, Ignacio would say, aggrieved, but I wanted to hear your voice, to know you were alive in the enigma of Chile. I'm alive, barely, but I'm alive, but we'll talk about what we've been thinking when we see each other again. I finally cut the conversation off, and when we hung up I wanted to cut my wrists a little, but I turned instead to my novel. The phone rang again. It rang and rang but no one answered. I was having a hard time finding where I'd left the handset, fumbling along the surface of the bedside table, bumping my long nails into the bottom of a lamp and meeting indiscernible obstacles until finally I found the phone. It had stopped ringing but I picked it up anyway, driven by the hunch it was Ignacio again, defeated by the anxiety that I myself was causing him, cruelly. I heard a Spanish accent, but it wasn't his. It was sprinkled with *h* sounds and strident *s*'s and with *z*'s so unmistakably *madrileño*. A rougher accent, much more emphatic than Ignacio's Galician, and it crossed through time and its turbulences. It was Raquel's hard voice talking to my mother's despondent one, trying to console her convincingly. With resigned patience. I'm sure, Raquel was saying, the operations are going to work. My mother stayed quiet for a moment, as if she couldn't breathe or it hurt her enormously. She gulped down air and dampened it inside her lungs, preparing her answer with the coldness she used when talking about the hopeless. Without seeing what was coming, Raquel repeated her candid *señora*, I'm sure, whatever happens she's going to be fine. Fine, I repeated to myself, overwhelmed by her certainty, unable to interrupt them. I let myself be carried along by those voices I knew so well but that were soon to become unrecognizable to each other. My mother let out an asthmatic whistle and said to her. You, what do you know? Are you an eye specialist? In the pause that followed I saw Raquel's disconcerted gesture, her immediate annoyance; I saw rocks falling from the ceiling onto her skirt. I thought about Raquel breaking her nails in that cave-in my mother had provoked. No ma'am, she replied then, drily, raising her voice just enough, I'm no specialist, I'm only a poet. And it's poetry that makes me sure. I heard the indecipherable stuttering of one of them, Raquel or my mother, or maybe what I heard was another conversation getting mixed up in the wires. Raquel? I said, because the conversation between them had died. Raquel, hi, what a surprise to hear from you.

militancy

Even now, even here, in this very passage, I confess it was not difficult to stop writing. It was much more arduous to find a pen, wrap my fingers around it, know that crooked words unreadable even by Ignacio were falling onto the page. Because as the world went black, everything that belonged to it was also left in the dark. Now there were voices that completed the unseen or that read to me tirelessly. I could fast forward or rewind them, interrupt them. Listening to borrowed novels suspended the anguish of not being able to write, it kept me from stopping to think about what I wasn't writing, about what I would never write. But now Raquel was on the phone, like a friend, like the militant poet she was, supplied with pens and notebooks to write down dark verses in microscopic script. Raquel called me to order.

What had I done with my unfinished novel? my general asked me. It must be thrown in with all my notes in some box from the move. While she waited, my mind went searching for the exact box in which I'd deposited the unfinished manuscript, the box that my hands had sealed like a coffin. I'd left the book half-finished and had no time frame to complete it. Raquel assailed me: at what point had I left off writing, how much more before I'd finish, and I couldn't remember. My memory was another blackout. It's impossible you've forgotten, she said, and I said nothing. You can't give up, she insisted, and I: it's not giving up, it's an interruption, a temporary impossibility. Did you forget yourself, too? Raquel hammered away, trying to activate my memory or my wish to remember. To remember not the forgotten pages, but the identity my blood had drowned. You can only be yourself when you're writing, said Raquel, as if she had to remind me, but I shot back—because this was a war and I needed to win a battle: maybe I wouldn't be Lina anymore, maybe I was backing up toward the abyss. Maybe I'd have to start all over again. Of course not, raged Raquel. Of course I will, I barked at her, consumed by an anger that did nothing but confirm she was right. I didn't want to start all over, I couldn't be someone else now, much less someone who was not a writer. It was just that paper and screens were now a disadvantage. The smooth keys that had been erasing my fingerprints for years were now an enigma. I couldn't even be sure it would be easy to go back to writing the same way once I was me again, if that ever happened. That novel is dead, I declared, and Raquel negotiated a maybe, maybe that novel is dead but there will be others. Because you don't write, she said, with just your eyes and hands.

So, for now, she added, as if giving her final order: right now, as soon as we hang up, start writing in your head.

dirt cheap

Ignacio was back in Santiago. Returning to a city he'd never set foot in. Returning like an unfounded rumor, like slander stuck to its victim for life. A taxi drove up very early to number 237. The door opened and first a foot appeared and second a leg and third Ignacio's skull and then two big suitcases. His left index finger touched the doorbell, and someone must have opened the door for him. He went upstairs and dropped his baggage thunderously. It was his way of announcing himself: making noise, making enough of a racket to wake me up. He was brought low by uncertainty and a silence he didn't know how to break. When he saw the swell of the pillow, he climbed fully dressed into the bed. It was criminally cold in the house and outside as well, under the dirty Santiago clouds, so thick the lightning couldn't pierce them; only the rain got through, acid and occasional. It was deadly cold and he was sick. A little sick, just barely. Performing his cough, his fever, exaggerating his stuffy nose, he mumbled an are you asleep? and then curled into me. He blew his nose harshly to finish waking me up. How'd it go? I said, still sleepy and realizing he was over-acting his cold. I missed you, he said, and his voice was that of a plucked bird perched on ice in the south pole. My feet are like rocks. Come here, I whispered to him, my breath thick: put them against me. And I let myself be embraced and I let him put his cold hands between my breasts, let him explode my ears in kisses, I even let him saddle me with his false flu, feeling an infinite pity for Ignacio. You should have stayed there, I told him. You should also have stayed there, he told me. That's true, I said, and here we are again, both of us. Like two idiots. Yes, what morons, but will you come back with me? Lina? I had to tell him yes, of course, because that's what I was going to do, but I couldn't compose an answer that was just right for him, not yet; we still had to finish sleeping and let the days and nights pass and the moon wane languidly. Why give definitive answers so soon? We would get out of bed in spite of Ignacio's theatrical shivers and the mucous in his handkerchief, and then he would open before me his suitcase studded with locks, like a treasure chest. It was a treasure bought *a precio de huevo*, as they say in Chile, dirt cheap: the price of an egg, but a rotten egg, an egg cracked in those days from the sudden Argentine bankruptcy. A *huevada* in the most Chilean sense of the word. A fuck-up by the politicians. A real shit storm, exclaimed Ignacio, indignant, moved, his cold getting a little worse. He'd gotten sick from anxiety and he coughed to clear it away, to clear his throat and convince me that it had undone him to see the city collapsed, but even worse to see its people digging rotten food out of the garbage. And not only the people who'd been miserable for ages and were more inured to disgrace and difficulty, but also the less prepared people, people who dress like you or like me, and he didn't mean his wrinkled clothes or my slept-in underwear but rather the everyday clothes of the people who can buy them; the whole social-climbing middle class who scrupulously handed their money over to the bank, only to be suddenly left penniless. Left with nothing but a pile of unusable credit cards and the change in their wallets. And with disgust but also with previously unknown greed, the corners of their mouths twisting into an incomprehensible grimace, drooling a saliva that smelled of hunger, they stuck their hands up to the elbows into garbage cans, or they posted themselves at the exits of restaurants to fight over the leftovers. It's an all-around collapse, added Ignacio between shrill sneezes. People are unemployed or have bad jobs or their salaries are frozen or they're simply waiting for payment that doesn't come. But people were still going to work, because it was better to wear yourself out than stay home sitting on your hands; better to wear out your eyes on the computer screen than doze in front of the TV, if they hadn't cut off your electricity yet for lack of payment; better to do something than stand staring into the empty refrigerator feeling hunger pangs. And then I, continued Ignacio, so scrupulous with money, who never buy anything I don't need and even less so now that we want to furnish the apartment, I who am terrified of ending up without cash in a foreign country…I, he repeated, talking as if to himself, I, who hold myself back from succumbing to temptation, from being consumed by consumerism (but sometimes you overdo it shopping, I thought, while you were making those declarations of principle). Well, I, I don't know what you're going to think of me, but I went out and spent everything I had. I blew the last cent of every dollar on me, I burned every Argentine peso treating complete strangers to beers or glasses of wine, and I paid the bills for people sharing my tables in run-down holes in the wall, in corner sandwich shops, in family-style steakhouses—because the Argentine cows aren't in crisis—and I wore myself out leaving tips. And it seemed as if he was nearing the end of an astounding epic tale, but then he added, almost without air, his throat contracted, his nose stuffed up, that he had done it all with the stupid idea of stopping the collapse. You alone, with just some dollars? Like a second-rate conquistador with glass beads? Yes, yes, you're right, I couldn't think of anything else to do, he said, swallowing. I couldn't help it, I went into stores like I was possessed and bought something, anything, it was all on sale, and the last thing I bought was this suitcase to carry all the gifts I was bringing you. I heard the sound of a *cierrecler*, a zipper, which Ignacio called a *cremallera* but some old Chileans with Arabic ancestry still called *marruecos*, and the metal teeth opened so Ignacio could take out all the clothes that had been "made in *la pampa*." He hoped I'd like them, even if only by touch. Because this one, see how soft, was a long jacket of sheep leather. One hundred percent Argentine sheep, cut and sewn by desperate hands. Chosen from among hundreds of jackets that the store clerks had modeled for him with the vanity of a different era. They were all short like me. And dark, *morocha*, he said, or as they say in Buenos Aires, *arrabales*. And they had very black hair and were plump in spite of or because of their poverty. And while Ignacio was talking about those girls modeling for a small sales commission, he handed me two wool sweaters and a pair of fleece-lined leather gloves and a horse leather belt that pleased my fingertips, and a shirt that felt like cashmere but wasn't. Merely cash, more like it, he told me. And it's all black? All black, he said, the blackest black you can imagine.

the use of newspapers

On the ice floe that was Santiago, Ignacio couldn't stop repeating it's so cold, my toes are frozen. His feet were like a cadaver's even with the hot water bottle and three pairs of socks. You don't use heating here? And yes, sometimes, usually we turned it on in the afternoons. Olga opened the doors and windows early to air the place out, and in filtered a winter that was impossible to chase away with a paraffin stove that, more than heat, exuded an infernal smoke. The currents of air sustained family life, they made us drop our little grudges to join in the accumulation of heat around the table or in a shared bed. But only Ignacio and I were in the house during the day. My brothers only appeared sometimes, fleetingly, on weekends. My parents worked continuously at their respective hospitals, consulting offices, occasional shifts and home visits. Aren't you dying of cold? Ignacio insisted, rubbing his hands together as if lighting a fire. I was trained to resist the damp air that was seeping into his bones. His teeth chattered. He got up from the chair and bent his legs to wake them up. He rummaged quickly in a packet of cigarettes, the match scratched in my ears, and I heard him suck on the cigarette in spite of his imaginary flu. I could envision him forming fragile smoke rings that his forced cough then tore apart, his dry cough and the beaten voice of a bellyaching Galician. Winter in my Santiago made him remember winter in his own, in Compostela, and he told me again how as a boy he'd slept beside a wall that let water filter in from outside, how he'd spent his whole childhood sick, covered in rashes, his ears hardened by chilblains. He exaggerated his hardships or invented them, all so as not to talk about our own. We need to move, he decided suddenly and predictably, putting an end to his moaning. But aren't you already moving? You're pacing like a prisoner. We need to leave the house, he corrected himself. It's colder inside than out. The car has heat, right? Yes, more or less, I wavered, at least there's heat from the motor. I want to buy another newspaper, because the one in the house isn't worth a damn. It used to be great for cleaning windows, I thought, and for wrapping eggs and fish at the market, but I let him transfer his climactic complaints to the newspapers and then I explained. Everyone says the same thing, Ignacio, here there are only opposition newspapers—that is, newspapers of the right. There are no left-leaning papers. Not even centrist papers. No newspaper that is informatively decent. Ignacio sighed. Where can we go? He got up again from his chair and immediately sat down again and crossed his legs. And then he let out an *uuf* or something similar, and he said no, we can't go, and he lit another cigarette, scraping another match. And, exhaling meticulously, he said, what a shame we can't go out. And why not? I don't know Santiago, he said, I've never driven in Santiago. And abruptly stubbing out what was left of his tobacco against the ashtray, he fell silent. What do you mean we can't? Of course we can, I'll direct you, I know Santiago like the back of my hand. I told him where to find the keys to the car that had once been mine and was still there, faithfully awaiting my return, and we went down, me limping a little and Ignacio trotting down the stairs that led to the door and the gate, and we went down also along expansive avenues that disappeared into the mountains until they reach, at the bottom, the rotunda that was one of the city's nerve centers. They killed a minister there,

I told Ignacio, pointing ahead without really knowing where to. They dealt with him in the first months of socialism. That was the spark of what would happen later, La Moneda in flames, the open wound of Chile's history. Yes, says Ignacio, who knows everything about politics but nothing about streets or motors. Ignacio who hates to drive, who now snakes through the city to save himself from claustrophobia. He accelerates so his anxiety can't keep up, and he heads west, following my directions. I put my memory on autopilot and I give him such precise instructions I surprise myself: keep in the left lane but stay on Costanera. Yes? It's the large avenue, and go a little further, a few blocks, and when we come to a wide street with three traffic lights with arrows and a left turn lane, keep going straight, and careful with the pedestrian crossing hidden behind some trees. And so we cross Santiago. Turn to go up, toward the mountains. I don't see any mountains, said Ignacio. They must be there, hidden by thick clouds from industrial smokestacks. And there on the corner must also be a sign. A little wooden sign. Do you see it? (Open your eyes wide, Ignacio, you're seeing it without seeing it.) Nothing, sighed Ignacio, exhausted as though newly blind himself. I don't see anything but a closed shop with the window covered in newspapers. Top to bottom, old newspapers singed by the sun. That was where I used to buy books, I told him, in a uselessly tragic tone, and then: go slowly because there's a speed bump in half a block. You see a big chestnut tree to your left? Then it's the next street, past a green kiosk. To the left is a parking lot. I hand him change. The cafe terrace will be covered in plastic and will have space heaters. Are we there? Yes, says Ignacio, his words thinning before a sneeze. We sit down to order two cups of coffee and to choose from a pile of worn-out newspapers.

painkillers

Lethargic, no schedules, no routines. We stayed in bed in the mornings like a couple of unemployed or retired people, or hopeless addicts, addicted to each other. Under the sheets we lived in a jumble of newspapers, cassettes, and neglect, of sleepiness and carnivorous groping seasoned with anti-flu medicines (Ignacio) and painkillers and anti-inflammatories (me). Ignacio was bombarded by an invented virus, and I, on top of everything, had shooting pains like needles in my groin. There were hours during the day, during the day but mostly throughout the immense night, when the stiffness in my hip intensified and I shuddered and twisted every time I turned over in bed. I lay still, assaulted by nails that drove into the joint and moved through my body, to come to rest in my insomnia. My mind raced until the fatigue of dawn. Ignacio's mind, on the other hand, fell into a coma from the medicine and he snored like he was growling; at other times, it was just a deaf and tortured whistle, almost a sigh. His was a sleep as restless, as exhausting, as my lack of sleep, and I wanted to wake him up to give him a little sex. Only a little, to get to sleep. Ignacio, I whispered, Ignacio, and I waited for a sign. From the deep pit of his consciousness rose a hoarse noise suggesting that even if he wasn't there, his body was indeed available. I started by putting my tongue in a corner of his eyelid, slowly, and as my mouth covered his eyes I felt a savage desire to suck them, hard, to take possession of them on my palate as if they were little eggs or enormous and excited roe, hard, but Ignacio, half-asleep or now half-awake, refused to open them, he refused to give himself to that newly discovered desire, and instead of giving me what I wanted he pushed me back onto the bed and put his tongue in my ear and between my lips although he didn't dare lick my sick eyes when I asked him to, maybe he was afraid or maybe disgusted, and instead he bit the nipples that were the open eyes of my breasts, and by then I had finished waking up too and I forced him back on the bed forgetting all my pains, and I kissed the start of his thighs, between his legs where it smelled of dampness and confinement, and I put in my mouth the tip of his body as if it were what most excited me, though it wasn't that exactly, not that but rather the knowledge that my tongue was moving under a thick eyelid of wrinkled and secret skin, to know that under that lid was Ignacio's blind, round, soft eye, giving in to me, growing taut on my tongue until it shed a tear, spasming, in my mouth. I drank the tear and I climbed up Ignacio's body to peer over his belly button and enter that socket as well. But Ignacio grabbed me by the shoulders, hesitating, still undecided about whether he should, whether I wanted it too, if it was possible, because between us, like a gash, was the doctor's warning, the medical words alerting us to the danger, Ignacio's terror of making me bleed again and making my eyes burst. But Ignacio, I whispered, that already happened, I'm already full of blood. Let's go for it, I told him, ready for anything. I said it like an extreme athlete tied to an elastic cord, ready to throw myself off a bridge of a not insignificant height, just to try my luck in the fall. But my harness was insecure.

But his heart was delicate. But pulled along by the strength of my impulse, Ignacio closed his eyes and clenched his teeth and begged me at least not to try any contortions in the air.

so I tell her, she said

And the door opened, pushed by an inopportune voice. May I? And it was Olga, her nasal undertone trailing a legitimate resentment toward the idleness of others. Her job consisted of cleaning and cooking, but there were unwritten rules: be available at all hours, sleep in fits and starts, get up at dawn to wake my parents with breakfast and the newspaper. In exchange, every day she undertook minuscule revenges that she justified as her duty. You two are still in bed? And she was beside us, loudly shaking out the rug. Come on, get up, it's ten o'clock. I'm not going to spend all day waiting for you. But you don't have to wait for us, Olga, we know how to make the bed, I said, finally opening my blindest eye, thinking, while I mentally told her off, that I was wasting my breath protesting. Olga would never concede to change the rules of the house, her rules, which she imposed with more authority than anyone when she wanted, and when she didn't, she shielded herself behind her old age. I make the beds in this house, she said, that's my job. It's what I get paid for, she added, opening the windows next to us without caring that we were sleeping or naked in the bed, clutching the edges of the sheets. Olga, could you give us a minute to get dressed? And what for? she said, utterly immune to the cold air. As if I haven't seen you in the buff since you were a little thing, you and your brothers and even your father, your dad who still wears those old pajamas. But Olga, that was ages ago, now we have hair, some of it gray, now we have rolls of fat, too-black moles, our feet are covered in callouses. Plus, what about Ignacio? Olga went on talking, making the most of that deafness of hers. She sounded like a preacher when she said, who bathed you all when you were little, huh? One at either end of the bathtub, I washed your hair, scrubbed you with the sponge, and rinsed you off, and then I dressed you. Your mother didn't even have the patience to feed you, she went running off to the hospital and left all her work for me. Because your mother was sure good at running off. As if the devil were after her. Olga accused my mother of foisting her work onto her, and secretly also blamed her that I'd left home so young, going first to a precarious room in a different neighborhood, then to Mexico and then Madrid on the pretext of writing, and finally to New York with the excuse of continuing my studies on a scholarship. And we were allies in our resentment toward my mother. Only I didn't resent her professional passion, I didn't hold her maternal distance against her during work hours; the impossible thing was how she'd brought the hospital home, how she'd turned me into her patient and my incurable illness into her personal disgrace. How she'd tormented me with her torment. How she'd never let me be her daughter, simply. To be her daughter I'd had to run away. Ignacio was still in a haze from the anti-flu medicines that he also took to help him sleep. A draught of air blew in. Lethargic, I pulled on the shirt I had within reach, but shivered when I stood up next to Olga, and I decided to get back into bed. No, she said, you two are getting up right now so I can make the bed and then, if you want, you can get back in it, but you can't stay in this mishmash of sheets. Haven't you seen how your mother gets mad at me for this mess? And I tell her it's not fair, said Olga; now that's really not fair. OK, Olga, I conceded, but give us a minute to get dressed. And she agreed but kept talking on her own from the other side of the door, raising her voice to be sure I heard her: and another thing I tell your mom, she said. If the girl wants to have a baby with things how they are with her, she should have it, I'll take care of it. Ignacio handed me a sweater while he buttoned his jeans and threw on his shirt, and it was me she was talking to. (Me but also you, Ignacio, about the babies, she was talking about the child that she wanted us to have so she could raise it.) May God bless you two with children so I can care for them. Babies, no, I said very much to myself. What I want are eyes, newborn eyes, nothing more. Yes, said Olga, pushing the door open and coming back in, as if she'd heard me and wanted to reply, you don't have to worry about anything. Plus, I know God is going to help you with this problem of yours. Cure her with your power, I tell him, and he tells me he will, he'll cure you if you believe in him. Olga was talking a bit to herself now, almost absently. I tell your mother that but she never listens to me; believe in God, I tell her, she went on, quoting herself. If she'd open her heart to God she wouldn't suffer, because God is going to cure those eyes of Luci's. That's what I pray for every day and night, that's what I pray for when I put potatoes in the pan and fry up onions, I even pray while I iron your father's underwear, Olga went on, a little out of it, why do you think I learned to read? So I could understand the Bible, honor God, so I could ask him for things. I even ask him for money sometimes when I need it. I know he's going to exchange those broken eyes and he's going to give you new ones, like they were just brought home from the store. And will I be able to pay for them on installment, interest-free? Don't go making fun of me, says Olga very seriously, you'll just see how what I'm saying is true, she says again, threateningly. You'll see, she says, pretending to be furious while I hug her.

will you two be ok?

In Santiago it's cold, but it's even colder at the beach. More knives in the air and words of warm vapor. More mold stuck to the walls and the window frames, more bars and wood to protect the glass from rocks. We had to get to the house and unwrap it, dust it, air it out, light the chrism of the little heater, dry out all the wet towels, the damp curtains. Same thing we'd done every time on arriving over the years. Sweep out the dead moths on the linoleum and the cow skin my grandmother had brought from Patagonia. Make the beds. See to the light and the water. My father drove the car the exactly one hundred and seventy-two kilometers of the Pan-American highway to Concón, giving all kinds of instructions to Ignacio that I also memorized, just in case. Following us for the same number of meters and centimeters came my mother, her brow furrowed, thinking who knows what thoughts that would wound like whips: the work it had cost her to be a woman and choose the trap of maternity, the anguish of having engendered a problem and not having known how to solve it: all of that would be making a deafening roar in her conscience while in the background, unheard, Beethoven's sonatas or maybe Mozart's would be spinning round and round. My mother and my father driving toward the same place in different cars so they could leave one for us. We'd have to be grateful. And we thanked them, so much, especially Ignacio. (Why thank them so much, Ignacio, why, since it was my mother and I who were going to owe you everything.) But don't thank us, dear, she said, it's the least we. And she interrupted herself, as if she went blank, as if bewildered, and then I heard my father, who saved us from that tight spot saying, ok kids, to the table, food's served, and then, when he saw me surely with my hair a mess and a lost expression on my face: Lucina, dear, fix yourself up a bit for lunch, huh? No, dad, there's no fixing me, but I ran my hand over my head, combed my hair with my fingers, and when I smelled the food I started to take an imaginary tour of our old beach vacations. I went back years in the vortex of time, catching balls of fuzz between my toes, and leaves, dust, sawdust, crust, salt, loose earth on the steep streets full of potholes, and through eucalyptus trees that the most ferocious winters later uprooted, I saw hundreds of sunsets swirling before my eyes. I wandered through those landscapes with steps I would have liked to be precise but that were instead erratic, abstract, steps lit by naked and hostile stars, steps that led me to beaches where I'd gone swimming, where the waves swelled crisscrossed with seaweed and thick foam, bilious, where I dove under and reappeared with my hair covered in garbage, supermarket bags, diapers dripping shit. And in the background some man hawking egg bread or wafers. I heard the sound of the chairs, the silverware. It smelled of just-toasted bread. And the same screen started to show my cousins sitting around the table before a hodgepodge of eggs, sausage, tomatoes, and mortadella on *marraqueta* rolls, eating with the hunger of the beach, bathing suits wet and hair stiff with salt, black sand stuck to their ankles, *señora* Alicia bringing in more cheese. These days the doors squealed, off kilter from the humidity, the refrigerator in its old age didn't keep things cold, the washing machine no longer worked. And the four of us lunched on grilled steaks with potatoes like the close-knit family we were but would also never entirely be. And then my mother offered instant coffee that only she wanted; and through the steam of the kettle *señora* Alicia emerged, fifteen or twenty years older. She pronounced my name with a *señorita* before it and there she stopped, maybe afraid, the soles of her shoes squeaking against the linoleum. She couldn't kiss me when I stood up, she couldn't reach; she'd always been almost a dwarf, and with age she had shrunk like my memory. There was so little distance between her head and the floor, but I had forgotten. It had been useless to bend over in search of her cheek's hard, shiny, dark skin, impervious to time. In search of her wrinkled fingers. Rather than try a kiss, she turned her back to me. She merely greeted me from afar, covering her mouth a little, and she shut herself in the kitchen to cry as if she were bidding me farewell. But I only heard of *señora* Alicia's sobs, like so many things, too late. I only understood the blows, the stomping, the fingers caught in the trunk of the car when my father stored a broken umbrella they'd bring back to Santiago with them. I preferred the tenacious pain in my groin, which spoke to me in a comprehensible language. It was a dry and crude warning, a concrete message with which to hold a solitary conversation.

I felt Ignacio's finger between my ribs. Your father is talking to you, he said. He's talking to us. Will you two be all right? repeated my father before leaving. My mother said nothing, she stayed quietly beside us until my father reminded her of the time. There was a salty wind blowing over the patio, over the unsettled tops of the pines, over our unsettled heads. My father honked the horn twice while the Dodge disappeared into swirling sands.

oysters without pearls

My memory's visual laws dictated the landscape to me. Screeching seagulls rose up over the esplanade, leaving a sedentary pelican run aground; they flew up along the sunset and then dove down, they drowned in eddies while the tide rose with the moon to cover the black beach. The moon was lost behind the trees; you could tell it was there, barely, from its shine. Judging by the light, Ignacio told me, the moon must be back there, and he took my hand to make me point my index finger toward a starry but dreadfully orphaned sky. But I couldn't care less about the moon, I was more interested in how the world's spinning on its axis was speeding up, how the wait was growing ever shorter. Ignacio recovered a bent cigarette and he smoked it slowly. I'm hungry, he said, blowing out the smoke. He felt like eating some Chilean shellfish. Why are you raising your eyebrows? No reason, I answered, lying, telling myself that if they hurt him I wouldn't be able to help. I directed him toward the fisherman's cove, bumbling along a road full of holes disguised in the night. It's so dark, Ignacio said, straining his eyes. Keep going straight, I replied indifferently. Where are you taking me? Is it close? Along the beach, after the oil refineries, turn left when you see the gas stations. The Oyster or the Pearl of the Pacific. There, I see it, cried Ignacio, and his stomach growled. That's where we're going. And when we got out of the car it was Ignacio who guided me, a rock, a step, now straight ahead, and the wicker chair pushed over the hard earth beneath me. The waitress. The menus. A plastic bread bowl, napkins. We ordered sea urchins, but they were banned. We asked for *locos*, but they were banned too. Oysters? We've never had those here. Lobsters? None left at that hour. What they had were *choritos al pil pil*, spicy mussels, and maybe a *choro zapato*, Chilean blue mussel, and since Ignacio was kneeing me I gave him a simultaneous interpretation: small and giant *mejillones*. And maybe some clams. That's all the seafood you have? Those and the fish, all very fresh, sir, said the woman, dragging out the *sir* in a trill. Let's get ceviche, suggested Ignacio. I ordered conger eel soup instead. We started to nibble a bit of hard bread and sip a slightly warm wine, and as soon as they brought our food I realized what I'd forgotten. (My purse. The syringe with insulin. I forgot it because I couldn't see it, Ignacio, but I also forgot it to put you to the test.) Ignacio went rushing out along the darkened road toward the prefab house with its red roof, and I sat smelling the steam rising from the conger eel without tasting it, patiently kneading breadcrumbs over the tablecloth. The waitress came and went, coming and going again, would you like me to heat up the soup a little while you wait? And I nodded so she would be entertained and stop spying on me, because the minutes passed and Ignacio didn't come back, he was lost in unknown neighborhoods, turning down dead-end streets.

But I didn't have any way to pay for the food if Ignacio didn't come back. I had no money for a taxi, I thought, which in any case you couldn't get around there; I didn't even have keys. There's your husband, breathed the waitress, bringing me the reheated soup, the fish now in shreds. And it was him, a panting, annoyed, hungry but victorious Ignacio whom I, sacking my memory, constructed in my mind: Ignacio brandishing the ampule of insulin like a flag that he planted on the table. I put my hand on the tablecloth. There was no syringe.

crosswords

Sloppy and swaddled in blankets like dogs, our ears cold, the tips of our noses damp. I opened my eyes reflexively and I understood I'd woken up, but I turned over again. A marine light was growing stronger in the hollows of the curtains, Ignacio told me, and then I finished waking up to tell him the light couldn't be marine, we were in the middle of a town, the house surrounded by dirt and pines that shed their cones onto the roof. Don't confuse me. Right, said Ignacio, and he tripped over a hot water bottle that had fallen to the floor like a dead child. He showered as fast as he could and I did the same, but I took longer trying to catch the soap and detect the shampoo. With our heads drying, we went out in search of lunch. Along the supermarket aisles Ignacio started hunting nouns on the cans of food—peaches were *damascos* and not *albaricoques*, peas were *arvejas* and not *guisantes*, beans were *porotos* and not *judías*. Then I stopped in front of a shelf, and moving my fingers softly over the surfaces like laser readers I told him that here cans are called *tarros* and not *latas*, and they hold *choclo* and not *maíz*. Don't talk so loudly, said Ignacio, and then, those are *olivas* you're touching. But are these *aceitunas* yellow? I asked. More like green, answered Ignacio. And afterwards we got in line at a register. And I know that in the afterwards of the afterwards the car stopped at a kiosk, that Ignacio got out, slamming the door, that he talked with the newsagent, held out his hand with coins on his palm and asked the man to pay himself, because Ignacio still didn't get the money. (That's how I remember it, as if I'd seen it with my eyes.) And still afterwards, Ignacio came back with the week's zillionth newspaper so he could follow in detail the crisis that was shaking the world outside us. Here, this is for you, I heard him say. I touched some booklets of cheap paper. What's this? I smiled. Porn magazines in braille? I felt Ignacio's laughter sticking to his voice: porn magazines for the blind that also work for people who can see, if they're trained. Schoolboys reading porn with one hand under the desk. And girls, I suggested, we shouldn't forget about them, discovering a voyeurism of the hands. Yes, said Ignacio, them too, the schoolgirls at public schools and private and catholic schools. Yeah, but what is this? Don't you want to guess? No, I don't want to, I go through life guessing, all this guesswork is killing me. Crosswords, he said, and me: crosswords? What do I want those for? *We* want them, Ignacio corrected me, so we don't forget words. Ignacio must have found my notebooks full of words in some box. Not books of grand quotations. Not titles of pending books and certainly not diaries. Single words that I collected so I could put them to work later on. Words that carried me from one idea to another with no need for a dictionary, which was a stopped-up dam of words. The crossword was a meaningless set of words that interlaced for no other reason than that they happened to share a letter. Sharing a letter as the only condition, I thought. Every word naked and crosscut with others in different positions. Are you sending me a coded message? And again Ignacio started laughing, inside and then out; he laughed in happy, booming peals that disconcerted me. I let him laugh because someone had to express happiness; and just like that, Ignacio laughing and me disconcerted, we went down, with the windows open, along roads that stretched like roots, letting ourselves be coated in dust and eucalyptus. We sat in the living room. Forget the walkman, said Ignacio, you're turning autistic with those recorded books, and then he announced: Clothing. Seven letters, and he plopped beside me like a wet rag. Apparel? Could be, and his pen wrote it down. Arabic liquor, four letters, it would have to start with an A. Arak. Govern starting with R, four letters. Rule? I heard the pen scratching paper, filling the empty spaces. You're not giving me time to think, Ignacio. Let's see, silversmith's tool used to change dimensions of an object. I have no idea what that is. Swage. Half a maniac? How many letters? If it's three, could be Man or Iac. Female Nobel winner with seven letters, under the photo of an old lady with really short hair? Mistral! And adding up words, we ate empanadas and drank a glass of wine, and still in bed it suddenly got very cold because the fuel had run out, and when he opened the door Ignacio exclaimed *joder*, the sun is coming up. But the word sunrise evoked nothing. Nothing even close to a sunrise. My eyes were emptying of all the things they'd seen. And it occurred to me that words and their rhythms would remain, but not landscapes, not colors or faces, not those black eyes of Ignacio's that I had seen spill out a love at times wary, sullen, cutting, but above all an open love, expectant, full of mirages that the crossword puzzle would define as hallucinations.

love is blind too

You'll see signs, keep north. Quintero. Puchuncaví. Zapallar. When the road forks, take a dirt road that will turn to sand that right away will be the blue ocean edged with pines, swarming with albatross, strewn with pigeon shit. With our feet sunk in the beach scum we walked—me, painfully—to the table where Genaro and the other man were waiting for us. Overcoming his aversion to awkward situations with a *pisco* sour in hand, and surely biting his tongue to keep from saying anything about how long it had been since we'd seen each other, Genaro hugged us both simultaneously. But sit down, he says, the clams *a la parmesana* just got here, and there's a bottle of white wine. Yes, echoes Genaro's lover, a delicious white wine. Ignacio pours me a glass that I grasp tightly in my fingers, and he moves the others so I don't knock them over with my other hand that flits over everything like a feather duster. I know Ignacio, Genaro, and the other man wield knives and forks like three musketeers and they attack the clams to which three steam- ing seafood stews are soon added, along with one or two reheated rolls. That, a piece of bread, is what I manage to chew, dissolve in my mouth, and swallow while they talk about people who no longer concern me. They swaddle the conversation with rigorous courtesy. They order another bottle and I drain my glass. And with the smell of salt and iodine encrusted in my nose I go back, now alone, to that long night when Genaro and I first met. The party where we'd been introduced, the immediate affinity, the emergency stairs where we went up the three floors to his apartment. Halfway up he stopped to explain. He wanted to tell me. Tell me anything you want, I said, wondering what that smell could be and thinking that it must be the floor cleaner. Tell me whatever you want, I repeated. And without altering the expression on his face Genaro told me that his boyfriend had just died of AIDS. Died in his arms like lovers die in movies, after a slow, terrible, unimaginable agony. He died without passing on the disease, but Genaro still suffered night sweats; he got up at midnight thinking about his own death. I remember that confession, and suddenly I understand that this lunch is a goodbye. Genaro will let me leave like he let the dead man go. And while I have this revelation, in my memory we're entering his apartment together and I see that the walls are covered in pictures the dead man painted. This is a mausoleum, I'd told Genaro, alarmed. You have to take all these down, give them a last kiss one by one before wrapping them up and sending them to a storage unit from where you will never retrieve them. That dead man won't let you breathe, he's looking at you from every one of these portraits. Genaro looked at me in horror, and then he looked at the pictures one by one, he stared at each painted face and he said yes like a zombie waking up, yes, yes, mechanically. Yes, Lucina, it's true, I hadn't thought about that, and he took down the paintings, he silenced their eyes, leaned them against the wall for a few days before putting them in storage forever. And he painted his house white again, he bought sheets

that didn't smell like the deceased man, and then he gave me all
the life he'd accumulated in those months of mourning. But then
I'd left him, I'd traded him for a doctorate in New York and for
Ignacio. Especially for Ignacio, who was so much like him. Genaro had taken me down from his friendship, he'd blindfolded me
with his rage, he had turned me toward the wall. This was only
a momentary truce. Here's to love, blind love, bellows the Genaro
present here, angry with wine, and I tell him yes, of course, Genaro,
we must always toast to that, and I pick up the only clam on my
plate and I feel like clouting him with it. I slurp the lemon juice
from the shell and push the mollusk covered in now-hard cheese
between my lips. Ignacio only opens his mouth to suck thought-
fully on a cigarette; his ashtray will be stuffed with broken butts.
I steal a drag, seeking Ignacio's comforting saliva on the filter, and
by the time they bring us the check everything between us has
turned salty and contradictory. The wind lifts up sand that the
humidity adheres to our necks. Genaro roars with laughter that
falls like a whip while he repeats that love is blind, that we are all
blind as clams, and how can we not realize. Not so loud, his lover
says discreetly, you're making a scene. But all the seeing people
are gone already, says Genaro, not a decibel lower. Be quiet anyway, that's enough. And then Genaro's lover turns to me, ashamed
(blushing, you'll tell me later, Ignacio). Don't pay any attention to
him, Lucina, don't mind him, he's been out of sorts for days, but
in any case you're going to get better, right? I'm quiet, annoyed,
thinking you're a cretin and at the same time thinking what not
to say; while I consider possible combinations, whether to console
Genaro or insult him, whether to be falsely polite to his lover or

throw the plates at him, I hear Ignacio start talking for me as if he'd forgotten I was there. We don't know what, he says, without finishing the thought. I snatch the words from him, saying that not even the doctor knows. But yes, says Genaro from somewhere, from all possible places, you'll recover like economies do, first up then down. Don't get started on the economy, I cut him off, tired of him and of the wind cracking open my skin and implacably lashing my hair over my face. What's more, Genaro, empires also fall and they don't rise up again, and it's getting really cold, it's time for us to go. Yes, Ignacio jumps in, prompted by my knee, it's getting dark and I don't know the roads well. We all get up at the same time and Genaro wraps me in his arms, kisses both my cheeks and my forehead, promises to call me next week, to come visit me, but I know he won't, that our friendship has ended in that picturesque restaurant of scavenging seagulls. We got into the car. They howled a duet of bye, Lucina, and they growled a ferocious bye, Ignacio, and I waved my hand slackly toward a place where no one remained. Not even the memory of Genaro.

darkened highway

And we headed back to Santiago on a highway where night had fallen at six in the evening. What did you think of Genaro? I asked, my bare feet over the heater. What about you? And the questioning stopped there. Already Genaro was crawling off with his lover toward the past that was a select social club; we were fleeing that closed circle, we were going forward and not looking back, we were present, hurtling into the future at hundreds of miles per hour along a road that had pretensions of being a highway. I opened the window and sniffed the air for the singed smell of burning. But there were no garbage bonfires at that hour. Not even flies. But we were traveling with a swarm in our heads, going back over conversations that wouldn't be repeated, anticipating situations. For an instant I had the impression that Ignacio was nodding, though I also thought he might be shaking his head no. I heard him shift ever more clumsily, felt him slow down sharply, put on the brake; I noticed we were zig-zagging. What's happening? Why are you speeding up and slowing down? It's pitch black, there's fog, you can't see a single light out there, and, as if that weren't enough, I can't see a damn thing in the dark. So don't go weaving in and out and passing cars. But I'm not passing, that's not it, said Ignacio, raising his voice. It's just that I don't understand a thing in this goddamned country, the road just melted into a high-speed throughway, and we almost ended up, just now, stuck under a wagon—a wagon pulled by cows on a highway! Explain that to me! Cows? I sighed, buying time to think. Cows or oxen or donkeys or idiot peasants or whatever you call those damned animals that almost killed us! They didn't have lights and they were going very, very slow through an impossible fog. And wait, *joder*, I can't believe it, there ahead of us is a truck right across the road, trying to make a U-turn! Are all Chileans crazy? Crazy, I murmured cynically, of course we're crazy, so better be careful with us. I must be even crazier, he said, shifting badly for the umpteenth time, braking, going around the truck's tail. Crazy to go on vacation with a blind woman. I bristled at Ignacio's head-on blow, but he started to laugh and that was his way, bewildering as

94

it was, of apologizing for the anger he felt sometimes, for feeling sometimes like a prisoner of the Chile that was me, and then I also started to laugh and cry a little from the laughter and above all from exhaustion. Ignacio went on reading the signs and driving in a straight line, and only when we were getting close to the city did I have to tell him what would be the next marker to look for, which exit, which ascent, which right turn to reach the house on a desolate Sunday at midnight. My parents were resting on their pillows, resting their skulls one against the other, their glasses on, the newspaper spread out, the computer propped against my mother's knees turned on. Asleep with the door open, whispered Ignacio. Olga was sleeping, on the other hand, locked in her room with the TV on full volume and the radio on as well. We reached the second floor and threw our sandy shoes as far from us as we could. We smelled of the ocean, of shellfish, of dirty socks, of Ignacio's sweaty feet. Are you tired? Yes, he said, exhausted. And then he lit a cigarette that ended up being for both of us, and inhaling slowly he started to tell me, between pauses, aspirating his words, how that afternoon. During that lunch. Between the clams and the *chupe de loco*. And the chopped onion and the *hallullas*, Ignacio, we can't forget those. Then, he said. Then? I asked. Then I started to think, he said. (What would it take for you to stop thinking so much, all the time?) It was nebulous at first and I kept thinking it more clearly after we went through the toll, while I was driving next to you, he said. The ideas wandered from one point to another, and I felt I was driving in the air. And then. Then the word *possibility* emerged. The phrase *the possibility exists*, although I know it's remote. Remote, I said, it's still remote. And I know, we shouldn't think about it, about this thing we've talked about so many times. Only that it's one thing to talk about it, I thought, and something very different to suddenly open your eyes. Ignacio went on laboriously, saying maybe. Maybe never. You understand? Yes, I answered, of course I do. You're the one who took a long time to understand. And I said to him, so what do you want to do? And without giving him time to answer I told him it was going to rain. There's going to be a storm, a torrential downpour. Can't you smell it? I said. It's in the air.

organize

Undershirts, tights with holes, threadbare clothes and dreams, skirts, unraveled cassette tapes, novels listened to and misplaced, and long hairs, bras, sheets twisted up on the mattress. And my fingers with their open eyes beneath the nails choosing and separating the clothes by material and size: the wool goes at the bottom of the suitcase because I'm leaving winter behind; on top the cotton and polyester fibers to bear the northern summer. I pause on each garment, reconstructing the memory of its stitches and zippers, sketching out where I got it or bought it, who gave it to me, what was happening when I wore it for the first time. I leave everything on the bed to settle for a few minutes while I shower and gather up the last of my things, the insulin and medicines for all my neurotic pains. It's only five minutes, or maybe ten—my time now is always approximate. Wrapped in a towel, I go back to the room and detect in the air the indescribable and unforgettable but always fleeting perfume of my mother. Mom?

What are you doing? Nothing, she says with a sorrowful voice. I called upstairs but you didn't answer. I came up to help you, your clothes were still on the bed, but don't worry, everything's organized in your suitcase now, she finishes with industrious maternal resignation. A silence opens between us that I fill with resentment. Those clothes, Mom, I say caustically, still wrapped in the towel. The clothes were already organized. I chose them and folded them and organized them myself with these hands, with these ten fingers that now have their own lidless eyes on their tips. You see them? Who? Who asked you? Who asked you to do anything? I'm barking at my mother, baring anxious teeth, I'm going to sink my fangs into her, smear her with bitter saliva. Kneeling on the floor, doubled over, agitated and angry, showing no mercy to my mother who has just turned into a trembling little girl. I look intermittently at her with my very blind and very wide eyes, and I grab the suitcase and dump it over the rug. I touch the clothes all unfolded, gravely injured, mauled by my mother and the perfume that reminds me of my childhood. I identify each article of clothing, slowly, in a silence full of daggers, and I again put polyester with polyester, cotton with cotton, denim with denim, then the wool and at the bottom, the Argentine leather gloves, the sheep leather coat, the belt. The boots. The impossible tapes of books that I'll never have the patience to listen to again. Everything so that afterwards my hands can find it. My mother is so quiet she seems to have stopped breathing, but I know, as if I were seeing it, that she's biting her lips until they're white. Finally from between them slips the word daughter, and then another aphonic syllable, without letters, as if my mother were so poor she didn't even have sounds to pronounce. But my mother has never been so poor she had nothing to say, and she says dear, I only wanted. To help, I say, finishing her phrase. To help me do things the way other people would do them. How I used to do them myself. But don't you understand? I go on with inherited insolence. I don't know if I'm going to get better. I have to learn how to be blind. You're not helping. But dear, my mother whispers as if to her own shadow, knowing that everything she says can and will be used against her. Your help invalidates me, I repeat, giving no quarter to my mother who is innocent but also, in a way, terribly guilty. She receives the stones I hurl at her like a martyr, and she starts to cry. It's a crying that is unforeseen and turned inward, a tense crying that includes all the miseries of life I've brought her. I hear her cry as I close the suitcase with all the clothes, the tapes, my slings and arrows inside. I get up from the floor and go over to her. I don't feel anything and it's better not to feel, better to simply let my fingers softly caress her face, her disheveled hair.

black box

(At night, headed north like weightless particles. Crossing the cloudy sky over the mountains. Cruising speed: eight hundred kilometers per hour. Ten or twelve thousand meters high. Minimum friction, minimum consumption of the oil that causes the wars you study. We were traveling in the pressurized and hermetic cabin unafraid of the windows exploding, or any bottles or our own circulatory systems. Cabins specially designed to prevent everything but thrombosis. Those seats don't induce sleep, and nor did the captain help, that loquacious pilot set on tormenting us with supplementary information: the height of the peaks and the cubic meters of pure water deposited in them, pure ice, he said, addicted to the loudspeaker. I don't know if you remember the stewardesses interceding with a rolling cart of drinks, after which we heard the captain return to the speakers to point out, stentorian, that soon we would head straight northward, that we would pass along the heights and the desperate depths of the Bolivian natives, before landing in Lima, where we could get off the plane or not. That no one should feel pressured to visit the mestizos at the duty free—do you remember? the *cholas* wrapped in their skirts—not even to find out how much they still hate, with deserved hostility, us Chileans. The laughter grated in the microphone, and with that he wished us good night for good. Finally, he shut up, you said, dozing from the cocktail of pills you'd taken for vertigo or air sickness, for your fear of planes mangled in flight, your black-box anxieties. You'd taken out pills for acid reflux and you'd also swallowed those, without water. You put it all in your mouth without disgust and before the stupor knocked you out, you carefully took off your glasses and asked me to put them away. Do you remember that, Ignacio? I covered that head of yours with the blanket, and I also covered my own. Ignacio, I whispered, and I blew on your face, and then raising my voice I repeated your name and squeezed your arm. But you didn't respond, you'd drugged your will away; you were as though dead, but a dead man who was completely mine. I rested your head on my shoulder and I went against the only rule you'd imposed on me. I was improvising as I went, running my fingers calmly, greedily, over your sleeping eyelids, feeling on my fingertips the soft touch of the eyelashes, feeling your skin opening and letting me touch the cornea, damp, rubbery, exquisite, and then my avid fingers ignited, they ignited but you didn't realize it, and I couldn't tell you now that I couldn't stop. I separated your eyelids and I ran the tip of my tongue along that naked edge that I felt like my own nakedness, and soon I was licking the whole thing, I was sucking on your whole eye softly, with my lips, with my teeth, making it mine, delicately, intimately, secretly, but also passionately, your eye, Ignacio, until the stewardesses came down the aisle imposing breakfast on us and I thought you would wake up. They left and then came back to take away trays, and little by little you began to resuscitate. I felt you stir, stretch forward, rescue a smile, and sink a finger into my cheek. How'd you sleep? I asked cautiously, and you said with nostalgia and presentiment that it had been weeks since you'd slept like that, so deeply, so happy not to be anywhere, forgetting about a wait that was still gathering. If only it weren't for your eye that was burning. It's so irritated I almost can't open it, and you cursed the plane's dry air with your voice still somewhere else, rubbing the eyelid a bit and putting on the glasses I handed you. The plane touched down lightly and slid forward. I, on the other hand, didn't sleep a wink, I told you, smiling with a sad happiness. I wove my fingers between yours and there we stayed, together, until all the passengers had left the plane and you stormed the aisle full of pillows.)

not the damnedest idea

Ipso facto, my mother would come. Not two days would pass, two or three days spent consuming another novel, me, and filling the refrigerator with food, Ignacio. But what am I saying? There was the work of preparing ourselves for the worst. Calls to the insurance company that doubtless would send us around in circles, to my thesis director to let her know my recovery promised to be long, the department head to put my registration indefinitely on hold, to the dean to beg him not to cut off my grant because I'd be left without insurance, and then. All delicate tasks, those and others we would undertake during those too-brief days in the muggy south of Manhattan. Visiting the eye doctor and bringing him an unlikely souvenir. Lekz made us wait while Doris demanded we fill out forms and hand over detailed descriptions of the situation in writing. I dictated to Ignacio. Yuku greeted me with her learned Japanese courtesy, but saved herself the bows before dropping in the paralyzing drops. My hand slid some fingers along the plastic petals of the plastic flowers in some pots of the same material, and returned to plant itself nervously on my knee while my body rocked slightly, forward, backward, like a tireless rubber doll. Stop doing that, Ignacio demanded or implored. Please, he said, stop rocking. I didn't know why I was doing it, I didn't realize I was until he pointed it out, maybe I did it to be sure I was still there, sitting in the chair. And I was still moving when Lekz came out of his office and approached me. He was standing in front of me, but he didn't call me by my name but rather said, ceremoniously and mechanically, welcome back missus…Missus, I repeated mentally, realizing he had completely forgotten my name. Follow me, he said, like a false missionary, missus…ashamed, not daring to ask. Lucina, doctor, I told him officiously, knowing he'd be unable to pronounce it, while I reached out my hand, but you can call me Lina. He doesn't know who the hell I am, I murmured then in Spanish to Ignacio, he doesn't have the damnedest idea, this doctor to whom I've handed myself over in body and practically soul for two whole years. Ignacio pinched my arm because Lekz spoke a little Spanish, in addition to English and Russian. He understood something because his wife, an eye doctor like Lekz, had been born in Galicia, like Ignacio. It was all true, his pinch and Lekz's wife's Galician Spanish. It was also true that my doctor did not remember my name. I smiled at him like an African doll, showing all my teeth, showing my tonsils if I had to, and I said again to Ignacio. Not the damnedest idea. Lekz must have already been deep in his illegible notes, because suddenly he seemed to remember and he said, surprised and happy, weren't you the writer? Aren't you in Chile? We were, for a whole month, corrected Ignacio, self-importantly. We saw the city, she showed it to me, it's not a pretty city at all, in fact it's pretty ugly, though it does have its corners, and he stopped, suddenly uncomfortable at seeming ungrateful. I ignored him; I'd been thinking about the word *writer* next to a verb in the past tense, the past of the books I'd written and that I wasn't sure I would go on writing. One eye would be enough, I thought for a second, until I felt Lekz's fingers taking my hand like a dancer and leading me on tiptoe toward the chair crowned with lenses. I opened my eyes resolutely and I let myself be looked at through the same apparatus as always. And from there I moved to the reclining chair and I leaned my head back, giving myself to the most potent magnifying lens, exercising my neck, preparing my ear to hear that the blood had not dissipated. There even seemed to be more of it, and it could already be coagulating. I think, said Lekz, with a slight cough, and I could imagine him stretching his lips into one of his Russian grimaces. I think, he said again without rounding out his idea, I think these malignant veins have gone on bursting. I think, he said, thinking again, that hopefully you aren't anemic, because the lack of iron would be an impediment to an operation. You will operate! I howled inside, you will operate, even if I'm dying. But Lekz went on thinking out loud, and next he asked, with calculated calmness, how have things? and I, without letting him finish, whinnied: good, very good, healthy as a horse, doctor. I'm full of energy, I could go to the operating room now carrying you on my shoulders. I'd carry you on my back or drag you, I'd take off running unchecked, wearing blinders so I wouldn't be distracted, I'd barrel past the signs saying do not enter, I'd break the window of the operating room, jump onto the cot, I'd separate my eyelids with my own fingernails so you could stick in the blades, I'd offer myself to the needles strung with thread so you could finish sewing me up. You'll need tests, he said, to rule out anemia. Tests! I don't want tests. I want you to operate. Right now. But Ignacio got tangled up in my arm and he dragged me off to the laboratory and when we got there, in spite of his sqeamishness, he stood firm beside me: roll up your sleeve and stretch out your arm. And I obeyed, swearing vengeance, and I made fists so my veins would pop. Ignacio's stomach turned when he saw how that blood of mine flowed, a blood that is always so like itself, my blood, like his but different only because it was mine, filling the tubes. And after the blood we went mutely to his apartment that was also my waiting room, which would be my mother's campsite when she arrived the next morning to interrupt the peace of the worried. Of course you'll have the operation, my mother reassured me as soon as she'd planted her high heel on the apartment's only rug and hugged me. Don't worry, dear, she repeated with absolute certainty, you have more than enough iron in you. They didn't have to bleed you to know that. Look at her face, she said to Ignacio, look at her fingernails, and she squeezed my finger. And then, without warning me, she stuck her long nail in my lower eyelid. She turned it inside out. She peered into it and said, you see, Ignacio? It's pink. That's irrefutable proof, she said, still not letting go of that insensitive bit of hide. Ignacio was taking nervous steps over the bare tiles, pacing to get away from my mother who went on saying, these doctors are so specialized they don't understand anything that's happening in the rest of the body. Only in the organ they study. They don't know anything. I agreed: they don't have the damnedest idea.

nightly bread

I can't eat, but who could feel hungry the night before? Dinner, no, but neither is it advisable to go to bed on an empty stomach. How about a slice of bread with butter that then becomes two: anxiety sets my mother's jaws in motion. I just salivate at the smell of the crumbs slowly charring in the toaster, the melted butter. She drinks tea, loudly stirs in two spoonfuls of sugar, takes a desperate bite of the toast Ignacio makes for her. I see it but I don't see it, it's as if I'd seen it: I construct it in my memory. It's good, says my mother, helping me imagine her every movement. Very good, she says, as if asking a question, and then she confesses she's eating purely out of vice. I'm not the least bit hungry, she insists, her mouth full. Ignacio makes more toast and my mother swallows it, and soon she asks, like a bulimic bird, is there a little more bread? And of course, there are two bags in the freezer, says my baker boyfriend. My mother burns her tongue on the tea but she doesn't get a chance to complain, because just then the doorbell rings and startles her. Who could that be, at this hour? Even though the hour is barely seven. Girl! screeches Manuela, who never managed to get past her youth, who still lives in the eighties, still in the student protests, running soaked from the water cannons and roaring with laughter, smoking joints. Optimism personified, absolute unfamiliarity with sadness. Manuela, my mom; mom, Manuela. And Manuela exclaims oh, I love the smell of toasted bread, plugging a kiss on each of my cheeks, squeezing my shoulders, giving me a transfusion of energy. What kind are you eating, *marraquetas*, *amasado*? Did you make it yourself? she asks my mother, who surely looks at her wondering where I've found this earthquake. In Chile, I answer her secretly, while Manuela says and I've just brought you some *paltas* as a present. *Palta*, repeats my mother, and she shrinks. Manuela stands behind me, and leaning over my shoulders she croons again a girl, how crazy, what happened to you! And right in my house, at that party, when we were having such a great time! Yes, I say, but I don't remember that happiness until she mentions it. I just stopped by to wish you luck, and she sits down next to me. My mother blows on her tea. Stay a while,

I tell her, we don't have any food, but coffee? Bread and avocado? I'm really not bothering you? My mother straightens in her chair, spreads butter on her umpteenth slice of bread, and continues to watch over me silently. OK! great! If I'm not bothering you of course I'll stay. I move over to the corner, Ignacio puts more bread in the toaster, and my mother chews on her thoughts. Manuela winds herself up and starts to talk about her new paintings and her new job, the one that pays her rent. Manuela couldn't import the small privileges of a Chilean artist when she came to this country, I explain to my mother. Just like the entitlements from the musty last names that here no one knows. That's why so many Chileans leave, says Manuela, maybe I'll end up leaving because of that too. I hear my mother abandon her silence, prompted to ask more about that new job. I take care of a little girl, answers Manuela. She's the daughter of a family in transition. In transition, I repeat, Ignacio repeats, my mother repeats with growing curiosity. In transition, Manuela also says, since the father discovered he was a woman. Who's a woman? asks my mother. The father? Exactly, says Manuela, and the father also discovered he is a woman who is only interested, sexually, in other women. That makes him a lesbian. So the girl has two mothers, I clarify, and Manuela laughs, yes indeed, and she adds that he or she is still in love with the girl's mother, but that she, his wife, who was fairly masculine and maybe wouldn't have had such a hard time getting behind the transition, decided to abstain. She wasn't ready to be with a woman, even though she'd spent years with her. Or him. My mother declares that she's now lost her appetite, but Manuela ignores her. She says: now he has to decide whether he's going to have the operation. Operation, echoes Ignacio, still making sure the bread doesn't burn, and mashing, I suppose, another avocado to keep his hands busy with something. Operation, of course, says my mother, in her knowing doctor's tone, while I hear her shifting in her chair. Manuela decides to give her the surgical details. My mother doesn't know if she wants to hear them, and I know Ignacio doesn't. He goes on mashing avocados, or maybe he steals off to the bathroom. I already know the details, and I also know the story's protagonists. The father's identity is a subject that used to interest me, but now I abandon the conversation to concentrate on something more concrete and definitive: find a crumb, a single crumb of toasted bread to calm my hunger. Manuela talks tirelessly while I reach out my finger very slowly toward the table, luring the crumbs my mother dropped and figuring the story would keep everyone's attention elsewhere. My finger crawls along the surface of the table, trapping one crumb after another. I hear Ignacio cough and I know he's looking at me that he's intrigued when he asks me, what are you looking for? Looking for? I snatch my hand away, retreat into my secret hunger and listen enviously to Manuela talking with her mouth full of words and bread with avocado. My mother groans, utterly full on the other side of the table, and she takes advantage of the lull to ask a question that's more like an impatient order, what time is it? Isn't it time for bed? But it's still early. Please, no one move. This is my farewell party. Manuela, says my mother very seriously and very alone but shielding herself behind the plural: we're going to have to ask you to go. Lucina needs her rest.

a cry

My mother asks for some covers for her bed. What about the sheet? But an un-ironed sheet wasn't enough, she asked for the heavy weight of a blanket over her small and gaunt frame. Mom, it's 30 degrees out, you'll fry. Not at all, replied my mother: she would sleep with the air conditioner on for that whole summer night. Mom, I charged again, profaning our familial hierarchy again, how could you? Have you gone crazy? The electricity bill will cost an arm and a leg. Or an eye. Oh, I know, and you've just lost your little student stipend, I know, you don't have to rub it in my face, said my mother without even a full stop in the middle, without breathing; the victim's guile spilling from her mouth as my ever-smaller mother dragged out her words and begged for her candy: if you don't give it to me, I won't sleep. I shrugged. Ignacio shrugged. My mother shrunk like a silkworm between the sheets and under our thick winter blanket. The living room went dark with her in it, hibernating. We went to bed too, but Ignacio tossed and turned and every insomniac somersault kept me from falling asleep. Talk to me about something, if you can't sleep. Ignacio hugged me and started to spew everything that was hammering at his brain, twisted nails, little needles, almost insignificant, the stingers of African wasps that repeated to him the following: would the alarm go off at five in the morning? Should we have ordered a taxi to come pick us up? Would my insurance pay my bills? Would there still be bread in the refrigerator for my mother's breakfast? But no, I said, discreetly moving my hand over his face, don't worry about her, she's easy to please if you follow her lead. Yeah? he started to ask, already dozing. Yes, she's so scared, I said,

and of course worried, he said. Yes, yes, I repeated, yawning, as if
it wasn't me she was worried about, as if the imminent operation
wasn't happening to us. Because we suffered that night without
knowing it. And, holding tight to trivialities, thinking about my
mother's anxiety and her easy happiness, we sank gradually into
the mattress, but soon the springs pushed us up again toward consciousness. We heard a cry. A high-pitched cry. A scream of terror.
A scream that lay like a cable through the night. And it came from
the living room, from the mouth, the larynx, from the strident
vocal chords of my mother. Did you hear that? I asked Ignacio.
Yes, I heard it, it just woke me up. It's my mother, I said. Yes, it's
your mother, he answered, with zero desire to get up. She's my
mother, I'll take care of it. I went sliding along the hallway, terrified
of finding a rapist, a thief, a hairy spider, or a snake tangled up
in my mother's legs. I held on to the walls, afraid I would bump
into her. Mama, I whispered, taking a step toward my childhood,
suddenly lost in a hallway before the Santiago bedroom where
my mother was sleeping. Are you there? Are you awake, mom?
I returned suddenly to New York with my bare feet at the edge of
her mattress. I waited for an instant, remembering how I'd asked
her the same question hundreds of times, separating her eyelids
with minuscule fingers in search of awake eyes in her sleeping
body. Mom. I said it again and filled my mouth with that word
that smelled of milk under her perfume. But it was that same
mother who had just torn through the night with her cry, who
had howled and woken us up but hadn't woken up herself, who
was now snoring gently, clutching the blanket. Mom! She didn't
answer. The inflatable mattress hissed under her dead weight, under

the imperceptible rocking that pushed out the air supporting her. The mattress was in motion, alert but unconscious or dreaming; just like my mother, I thought.

I can't tell you

The first sound was of hands taking dry plates from the rack and depositing them in cabinets. Then came other noises. Stuck wooden drawers that shut suddenly. A broom sweeping dust balls accumulated in corners. A household symphony conducted with a vocation for order—one my mother didn't tend to exercise in her own house, but always in mine. Once her anxious work was finished, my mother decided to knock on our door. She turned the knob but couldn't open—it was locked. The floor creaked under her feet. She must have been leaning over, her ear to the hinge, her mouth on the wood singing an are you awake? with a thread of a voice that sounded frayed, about to snap. The loose floorboard creaked again. Feet. Manicured toenails. Slippers. Isolated words of my mother's under the shower and then, repetition of the scene in reverse. The bathroom door opened again, my mother came back down the hall and stopped, trying to crack our door open, and by then we were awake. Ignacio reached out an arm to turn off the alarm, I reached out another to find his face. My hand touched Ignacio's lips, Ignacio's nose, his eyebrows, and for a moment again, fleetingly, his eyelids. I felt the tense bags of his dark, tender eyes while Ignacio squeezed his eyelids for an instant and in one leap was up. I rose after him, slowly. But Ignacio was standing still, sounding out my mother's presence in the hallway and, when he didn't sense her and saw that I didn't either, he opened the door and we went out, goaded by fresh, confused thoughts. I slipped into the bathroom with him and while we brushed our teeth, an entire night of dreams began to swirl in my head. Strange dreams, full of buttons, I told Ignacio as we took turns spitting out toothpaste. Don't tell me about them, he said indecisively, drying his mouth, I'd rather not know. I smiled while I climbed into the shower, remembering some enormous buttons sewn to our bodies, buttons sewn with fishing line, with hooks, fish hooks, yes, even hanging from our ears, buttons, while I heard him, Ignacio, ask me. So, about your dreams? His voice from the other side of the curtain, waiting for me to get out so he could get in. Were your dreams in color? The water sloshed in my soapy belly button, ran over my neck, splashed my warm back, but those weren't the kind of dreams I'd had. Dreams of feelings and shapes, unseeing dreams. Maybe, I said, just to say something, anything, because suddenly I was overcome by the awareness that I was going to have an operation, and in just a few hours. And I started to wonder what my eyes would be like afterward, if I would still have them when I left the operating room. I threw that waking nightmare at Ignacio, and I also flung it at my mother, who immediately answered, in a typical outburst, but why would you leave the operation without eyes? What makes you think that? she said with preoperative nervousness, all to avoid saying to me what she said to everyone else: and what do you know? Are you a specialist? Mom, I told her, answering the thoughts that reached me telepathically, I barely know what my own hands are doing. I can't trust in the hands of others.

no man's land

At this hour the city is in a coma, but as soon as dawn comes it's unbearable. It was Ignacio talking. There's not a soul out, confirmed my mother, looking back over her shoulder; my mother, always terrified of walking down a street empty of people, empty of barking and honking, under the light of opaque street lamps. She feared the dark street, not realizing the danger lay elsewhere. I thought of her pupils, blurry from astigmatism, sunken in the dawn. I thought of Ignacio's myopia behind his lenses, Ignacio ever more mine, fumbling along the dark sidewalks. What a fantastic trio. My mother glued to me, me glued to Ignacio. And she was saying and this is, a…beginning the phrase and then breaking off. A wasteland? Yes, she nodded, a wilderness. An empty or barren place, I said. Yes, it's true, said Ignacio, we're in no man's land. This is the border between two worlds. My mother said no more. She clutched my arm as if I could protect her from her fears. We went on walking. I sank into my own words while they plunged into theirs, all of our shoes echoing on the cement, hurrying up the stairs to the rusted rhythm of the rails, sliding into an almost-empty car. And we went nodding with the same worried drowsiness to the 14th Street station. The first morning lights would be sneaking out above a city that flowed noisily around us on the streets. There were also the police whistles, the howl of a distant ambulance. Here it is, announced Ignacio, and there it was, I thought as I called up a memory: on that corner, the small, brick hospital founded to treat only eyes, only ears. The history of my eyes was archived there. In the hospital's underground memory lay hundreds of splendid images of ruin. I sat in reception pressing my fists against my temples, knowing they were going to operate on me but that no cure existed. The illness would remain, no matter how they opened and shut me. And even if I got my sight back there was always the possibility my veins could stretch out again; the blood could always spill again. My rush to throw myself on Lekz's knife lost its momentum; this was the choice, the bet on the Russian roulette. I had to bet to prove myself to my bodyguards. They had faith and picked up their pace, wandered in rooms under sinister florescent tubes and hallways crawling with Filipino nurses with Spanish last names. As soon as they handed in the papers certifying me as damaged and Chilean, they came back bearing new instructions. They said let's go, let's go, they wore brave faces, let's hurry or we could lose our turn. Let's go, let's go, what are you waiting for? they said in a duet, with the solemnity of a Greek chorus. I'm the heroine who resists her tragedy, I thought, the heroine trying to drive destiny crazy with her own hands. But not yet, I went on thinking, we have to give the doctor and his medicine a chance. Let's go, I replied, giving in, not that there was any way to resist. Not now that the cards were dealt and the insurance brought up to date, not now that I see no way to go in a different direction. And I know that my mother was glad and Ignacio somewhat intrigued when I smiled. And then I went up some stairs and down others, and then we went down in an elevator full of blindfolded patients, lying on cots or sitting in wheelchairs. Smiling. (That's what your eyes saw.) And we took steps in different directions. Here it is, said Ignacio. There it was, smelling of disinfectant.

what eye?

Begin protocol: take off your clothes, put on this flowered flannel robe, tighten these too-baggy pants. Now we just need the plastic cap. You look beautiful, cries my mother. I adjust the cap while she adds, you look just like a little girl. Mom, I tell her, arranging my hair under an elastic band that's come unsewn, you mean I look like I did when was little? I don't remember having even a moment of childhood. Not an instant of calm. Not a second when I wasn't wondering when the hand of tragedy was going to touch me. My mother doesn't answer, she makes a face, she bites her lip with total confidence. I keep trying to get my hair up under the cap, thinking, why it is that when I ask questions no one answers me, telling myself I shouldn't answer either, now that the interrogation is starting. Filipino voices with cutting accents. One asks me who I am, what my name is. I give my full name, I spell it out. My mother confirms that is the name I was baptized with. Ignacio verifies that it is written correctly. Someone else takes my arm and fastens on it a plastic bracelet that gives my prisoner's alias. I get up, I sit down. It's cold, I say, but now no one responds. Another voice intervenes. What is your name? it says. I hear typing while I answer, afraid of making a mistake. And then, any congenital illnesses? What medicines are you taking? How many hours since you've eaten? I don't know and I don't want to know. Did you go to the bathroom this morning? I hope so. What are they going to operate on? Which eye first? The voices change but the questions are always the same: Which eye will the doctor start with? With my mind's eye. Have you had any operations before? Yes. Any metal plates? Maybe. And what's your name?

Spell your name, did you sign your forms, all of them? What forms? The authorization to film the operation. Film it? Yes, we need to have it, for your safety, just in case, to protect you. Any allergies to any medications? Any previous surgeries? What is your last name? Which eye will they operate on? This one? That one. Any false teeth? Maybe. Contact lenses? Your last name, your first? Did you sign? Married or single? Which eye will go first? Tell Lekz that I want a copy of the video, I tell the voice of the moment who answers: do you have AIDS? Have you had any venereal diseases? How many lovers? So many? Women or only men? Tell the doctor I authorize it but I want a copy. Stable partner? That I want a copy of the recording, yes, they say, now we're asking, are your parents alive? Are you pregnant? How many units of insulin per day? The doctor sent me to ask why you want a copy of the movie. Why else would I want it? I ask, to watch it when I can see, with my own eyes or with Ignacio's. And are you wearing any rings? Why are you here? To supervise the maneuver. Height? Allergic to penicillin or any sulpha drugs? Any painkillers? What are they operating on? Any allergies? The permission to record the operation, did you sign it? But will they give me a copy of that beautiful and repulsive tape, covered in blood? Any metallic prostheses? All of them, I'm a bionic woman, with titanium eyes, and I laugh to myself, aloud, asking in return, asking the air, who was the one with the expensive telescopic and infrared eye? The six million dollar man? Is he with you? Who? What eye? Which one? Are you sure? And what insurance, what plan? How many children do you have? Any induced or illegal abortions? How many? Which eye? And the second? Did you sign the papers? Right or left?

The permission to film the operation? What is your name? Who is your doctor? Spell. Which eye are they operating on? One or both? Social security number? Last name? Mine or the doctor's? Any chronic illnesses? What medicines? Units? Grams? How much do you weigh? Who is with you? How old are you? Authorization of the operation? The document releasing the hospital from any damages? Are you left or right-handed? With which hand do you sign your name? What is your real name? Any pseudonyms? What do you do for a living? What is fiction for you? And damages? What do you mean by damages? True or false? Which eye first? Does it hurt? Why do you keep pointing at it? is it this one? this one? or this one? And you, who are you? Whose cap is that? And the eye, whose is it?

pure biology

Still breathing in that salty scent stuck to his shirt. Holding onto him, I kiss his mouth and his cheeks that grow gaunter every day, the corners of his eyes. A strange happiness moves through me when I feel the edge of his eye twitching under his skin. His living eyes. Ignacio pushes me away and plants a kiss on my ear. My fingers climb up his face again but Ignacio says please, don't do that. He puts his temple next to mine, and again the happiness overwhelms me, the happiness of having an instant of his body for myself, just before they make us separate. What will you two do while I'm in there? Silence. A silence that keeps me from guessing what gestures are made, what faces. What will you do with so much time? It won't be so long, says Ignacio, distraught, knowing that he'll have three whole hours alone with my mother. Four, in the worst case scenario, two hours per eye. I understand that he's repeating this to calm himself. According to Lekz, says Ignacio, he's never spent more than four hours fixing a pair of eyes. He said it could even take less, if he hurries a bit. Don't worry, adds my mother (I see her through your eyes, Ignacio, comforted to have company, fixing her hairdo), don't you worry, dear, we'll find some way to entertain ourselves. And she said it as if saying: alone at last. My mother will have Ignacio to interrogate, she'll have him especially to besiege with those medical stories he hates so much and that I grew up listening to. Stories of medical errors, stories I'm addicted to. Ignacio holds me tightly and starts to tremble a little, he squeezes me, wrings me out, suffocates me; don't leave me alone with her is what he seems to be saying. His heart speeds up. Anxiety heightened to the nth degree. But I, his shield against my mother, his defender and his secret torturer, I can't protect him now. Let me go, Ignacio, I have to leave. Don't be a stranger, he says. Here's hoping, I say, and I raise a white cloth in farewell while a nurse's soft hand takes my arm. It's the hand of a Filipino woman who speaks to me slowly. And, seduced by her malignant voice, I let myself be led to the place where they will sacrifice me. She helps me climb up on the operating table. You won't feel a thing, she assures me as she stabs me painfully with the IV needle, followed by the anesthesia needle. I lose my head with so much needle in my vein. Are you ok? she asks, and my being, this *Chilena* covered in a ridiculous flowered robe, tells her, pronouncing the words with difficulty, no, not at all ok, this table is very cold. Before I finish my complaint she throws a blanket over me, and the heat relaxes me, puts me to sleep. My new Filipino girlfriend takes me by the wrist, searches for my pulse, and breathes a what's your name, what are they operating on, which eye first; but I've forgotten it all, I don't know who I am and I can't explain why I'm there in her arms, I only hope that she knows the answers in spite of her questions, that the questions are just a strategy to distract me from my teeth, which are chattering now. And I realize, because I recognize his throat clearing, that Lekz is now behind my head, that those are his hands straightening my head, arranging my cap, washing my corneas with a creamy cotton. I also realize that next to him is another oculist I remember vaguely, because she works in the same office as Lekz, because she is, I remember now, his wife. She's going to assist him in the job. All in the family, in here and out there, I think, without retaining the thought. And maybe it's my nurse who tells me to reach one finger up toward the ceiling, a finger of a hand that now weighs a ton and soon dissolves. The finger is no longer there. My hand isn't there and neither is my arm. I'm not me anymore. Lucina vanished, her being is suspended somewhere in the hospital. What is left of her now is pure biology: a heart that beats and beats, a lung that inflates, an anesthetized brain incapable of dreaming, while the hair goes on growing, slowly, beneath the cap.

hours

This was seen by other eyes. How, from that first minute, Lekz fastened my eyelid back to keep it open. How he peered into my distended pupil. How he opened three holes in a triangle, one above, one to either side. How into each hole he inserted a different apparatus: a wire topped with a very strong magnifying lens, a multi-functional pincher that cut veins and cauterized wounds, and a light cable to illuminate the retina. Three metal filaments acting together, to prune and burn and patch for many more hours than the promised three or four. And this was seen by eyes not so far from me. How, while I was absent from myself, Ignacio and my mother fled the waiting room. How they went out to take a walk around the city, and, sick of wasting time, they went into the dive on the corner, shared a pizza and a warm coca cola, and smoked hurriedly from the same pack. The operation must be almost over, they said to each other in encouragement, walking hurriedly back. They sat in a hospital hallway and, obliged to carry on a conversation, they took out and polished their worst memories, one by one. How my mother had survived three mistaken diagnoses in a row: a sharp vertigo that was thought to be multiple sclerosis, a terminal brain tumor, an attack of intestinal colic interpreted as cancer. All errors that could have been fatal if they'd been true, she said—the victorious survivor, my mother—but they were only spots on x-rays. How Ignacio turned pale, because hearing about an illness made him experience every one of its symptoms. How anything could happen, my mother consoled him, but he shouldn't worry, now he was part of family of doctors, now he was protected from diagnostic errors. People used to think, my mother went on, changing the subject a little— though not much, only shifting the conversation so she could tell another story that Ignacio would rather have been spared: people used to think that Alzheimer's was a form of dementia. That's what my mother had! interrupted

Ignacio, connecting again in to the conversation. Dementia? No, Alzheimer's. And my mother took advantage of that revelation to gather information about his family's DNA, bombarding him with genealogical questions, drawing conclusions. So no one knows who your grandfather was? said my mother, taking mental notes, telling him that she had also barely met her father. What a coincidence, Ignacio told me she told him. Coincidence that my mother and his mother had only seen their fathers once. My mother to say goodbye to him when he was in the mortal throes of cirrhosis; his mother simply by accident. The two mothers had also coincided in their refusal to call the stranger before them father. Mine told her father, she told Ignacio: You are nothing to me. His told her father, and then Ignacio told my mother: I don't know you, I only have a mother, and she's more than enough for me. They confided so many stories, but with all the time they had, even family began to run out. Then they only stared at the time: my mother at the dead hallway clock, my Ignacio at his uncomfortable wrist watch. They took turns going out to the street to take drags from the last cigarettes, exhaling the smoke against the sticky windows. And whoever stayed inside just watched the parade of patients leaving the operating theatre escorted by Filipinos. But fewer and fewer patients were coming out, and the doctors must have been scurrying out through other doors. Janitors multiplied, armed with brooms and mops. And there they stayed, my mother, my Ignacio, watching the second and the third and the fourth hour pass, no longer knowing how many had gone by. They sat and stood, paced around the room, annoyed, downcast, drinking infinite coffees from the machine. No one came out to give them explanations, because there would be nothing to say until the operation ended, and the operation ceaselessly stayed its course. Lekz didn't make time to send reports to the outside. He couldn't have done it even if he'd had the time. He didn't do it because he couldn't see anything with his eye up against mine, so full of blood. He didn't dare lift his gaze. He wouldn't have ventured to blink, neglect the exact movements of those gadgets that lit, magnified, cut, and burned veins, possessed of a ruthless voracity. He had to control the energy in his hands, fear those feet of his, stiffened from so much pushing the pedals on the floor. Because hands, pedals, and feet, said Lekz, on finally leaving the operating room and finding Ignacio and my mother, who ran toward him as soon as they saw him; pedals and pincers, he said, pale from hunger, green from exhaustion, those instruments, he said, are not extensions of my fingers. They have life of their own and are ready, at the slightest slip, to yank a person's sight out at its roots. Ignacio looked at my mother, who didn't blink as she looked at Lekz, who was clearing his throat to add that once he was finally able to extract the viscous gelatin of blood that was my swamped vitreous humor, once he could finally examine how my right eye had turned out, he'd shuddered. But he told himself, he told them, right away, that he had to take advantage of the adrenaline, and he threw himself headlong into the left eye. He cut, it spattered, he cauterized and meticulously vacuumed the bottom of the eye until his arms started trembling. He washed his hands from the nails to the elbows, he rinsed his face and felt his nostrils vibrate, he dried the nape of his neck, but Lekz didn't dare issue a verdict. Much less think about one. It was worse than we thought, he confessed, drawn, and he used the plural because his assistant or auxiliary or wife was behind him, still in scrubs, displaying the same monumental circles under her eyes. I have no idea, not the slightest idea, he repeated. To my mother. To my Ignacio, who also looked exhausted from the work of waiting. There was nothing to say about the future. Lekz proceeded to go back over what had happened inside my eyes, over several months. My mother listened, utterly hypnotized. Ignacio was utterly ill. His knees went weak, he staggered toward a corner, and without anyone noticing he'd gone, he pressed his slippery hands against the walls, listening, as though from a distance, to a muffled voice wafting in through a portal to the medical hereafter: we would have to wait another twelve or eighteen hours to know if Lekz had left me definitively blind. That means? my mother, her voice also a distant whoosh, wanted specifics. It means that if she sees light tomorrow, there are possibilities, intervened the assistant wife. If she doesn't see anything, the doctor broke in, scratching his neck, stretching his shoulder blades like a tattered bird; if she doesn't see anything, I don't know, ma'am, we'll just have to see. *You'll* have to see, Ignacio told me he thought, now lying defeated on the floor. You'll have to see, he repeated to himself before insulting Lekz very Spanishly, *la madre que te parió,* fuck the mother that bore you, and all doctors, while you're at it. He put his dizzy head between his legs and that's where he left it. His mother had advised him to do that when he was a boy; his mother, who wasn't a doctor or a nurse and who knew no other work besides housework, his mother who had always been illiterate and was now very dead. Lower it. So you don't faint. Take off your glasses. Breathe very deeply and hold your breath. Like that, his palms still on the floor tiles, Ignacio heard Lekz drag his feet as he moved away down the hall, and he also heard my mother's high heels echo as she approached.

refrigerated chamber

I'm all patched, with a bandage over each eye fixed with adhesive tape. My fingers have just woken up, and they feel about the edges in search of a corner they can peel away. A severe hand intercedes, and there at the unstuck edge a prohibition falls. Ignacio? Let go of me, Ignacio, my face is burning. But Ignacio doesn't let go and I repeat, take this mask off or I'll take it off myself. Without raising my voice, without even hearing myself, I ask again if those skinny but strong fingers are his, that rough cheek, the mouth that kisses me almost without touching me. I ask him, with no compassion. Do you still love me, now that I'm your mummy? If you love me enough, stick your finger under these patches and make sure I still have eyes. Maybe I'm having this conversation with myself, maybe I still haven't woken up and I'm still immobilized in a nightmare. But in that sinister place I hear myself whisper again, with increasing awareness, with growing fear, what happened in there? Do I still have eyes under here? I hear myself clearly, begging Ignacio to let me be sure they're still in their sockets, that it hadn't been a mistake to blindly sign those documents. I wonder how long I've been absent from my life and the lives of others. It's late, says a muffled voice that could be his but could also be my mother's. And then I fall into another pause, from which I recover to ask again about the doctor. He'll be here tomorrow, they answer with unexpected clarity and in unison, my Ignacio and my mother. Tomorrow morning, she says. Stop touching your face, he says. But my skin is stinging and so is the uncertainty and my entire body feels like running away. Let's go, I say resolutely, but no one moves. Not yet, replies my mother, and in a fluty voice she announces the nurse's entrance, who in turn confirms that I'll have to stay. Stay the whole night. With someone. I'd rather be alone with myself, I want to say, but the nurse perforates my mouth with a thermometer; she listens to my heart above the sheet, she strangles my wrist in search of a pulse. Which of them is going to stay with you? the nurse asks again, but I, with my mouth occupied, can't answer. Ignacio raises a hand. My mother raises another. The contest between them begins. I keep my lips tight around 36 degrees while the nurse certifies it in her file, not watching the scene in which they, after having confided family secrets, now compete like strangers to spend the night in a reclining chair. My mother throws out the word newcomer, Ignacio parries with the word baloney and says anyway, let's see what Lina says. Tie, I respond. You should both go. But instead, out comes a coin that contorts in the air, showing its head and then its tail and then clanging on the floor. Ignacio leaves and heads straight for his insomnia, and my mother announces that no matter how tired she is she won't be able to sleep a wink. She promises to watch over me while I sleep, but as soon as she leans her head against the reclining backrest, she's asleep. I hear her heavy, her slow breathing. A hellish night begins, which is anything but hot: the room is a chamber refrigerated by the metallic buzz of hundreds of ventilators. The blanket must have slid to the floor, and I shiver under a steady stream of air. I can't get out of bed. I'm attached to the saline bottle that's hydrating the blood in my veins. They haven't left me a bell to ring in emergencies. That's what my mother is here for. Mom, mom, mom, repeats my echo in the hospital abyss. Momomomom, I say again, raising my voice, directing a resentful but contained damned old lady her way. But my curse doesn't shake her, my rousing call doesn't move her, my fists scorching the side table, my kicks in the bed. Not even her own damned snores wake her up. Not even a far-off, intermittent hiccup that also disturbs my night. I scrawl a message with the toes of my now-frozen feet: If I die of hypothermia or pneumonia, may someone accuse my mother. In abject desperation I decide to seek consolation by unsticking a corner of the patch and letting the night slip in under it, along with my finger that reaches in search of my eyelid and finds it. There is a dozing, convalescing eye. One eye next to the other, with small bumps that hide knots under the eyelids. And it's already dawn when someone comes in and I beg them to take my mother away and cover me up while they're at it. I lose my senses under the blankets, and then we reunite. Awake and still bewildered, the three of us again: my mother complaining about how she didn't sleep, Ignacio drawing out his vigil. There we are, a sleepy trio, sitting on the bed like castaways, waiting for the doctor.

bubble theory

If my fingers had been slowly pulling at the edges, his finished pulling it off: in one yank, off with the first patch, and another yank for the second, tearing out my eyebrow hairs. We were sitting face to face for the zillionth time, the doctor and I. Open your right eye, was the first thing he said to me. And the second: Do you see anything? I sat for an instant thinking about his question, thinking that I didn't know how to answer what he was asking me. I was a tremor, right down to my pupils. Now, repeated Lekz, more slowly and articulately, as if he were translating: Do you see anything? If I was taking a long time to answer it wasn't because I didn't understand the question, but because I'd been trapped in the very center of the verb. See something. See what? I don't see anything, doctor, I murmured. I was dazed or blinded by a vision of eternal life in the precise instant of death. I only see light, doctor. A white light so bright it stuns me. That's all. No shadow, no shading, not a single object. Uh-huh, murmured Lekz between his teeth, and then he muttered a curt good that for an instant struck me as the opposite of what he was saying. *Good* was a word Lekz sometimes slid out like a crutch, and other times it seemed to weigh heavy on his tongue, like a rock that sinks in silence, leaving only ripples. The word had an expansive effect in the room. Because there were other people there besides us: my mother who sighed and my Ignacio, whose clothes hissed as he shifted in his seat. Lekz continued his examination: he lit an electric moon inside my eye, illuminating my most perverse desires. And what do you see now? he asked, still pointing his flashlight at me. Only immaculate light, doctor, no more. That is, even less than before. But unshakeable, undaunted Lekz said, and now? In the left eye? The doubled light was exhausting me. I wanted to close my eyelids, both at the same time, and return to the refuge of darkness. That light illuminated emptiness, solitude, my absolute helplessness.

I'm still blind, doctor, but now everything is white. I sensed my mother standing up from her chair when she heard me, Ignacio uncrossing a leg. How Lekz ran his hand through his mane of hair in search of his future baldness, all to tell me that this was good, dragging out the vowels; how the best thing, for now, was for me to see just that. Lekz had emptied my eyes and fill them up again with helium. That was what I was seeing, then: two balls of gas in which the light converged. I inflated your eyes and now they're pressurized. I had no other choice, said Lekz somewhat solemnly and abruptly, and then I sewed up all the holes by hand. You'll be feeling like your eyes are going to explode, like the stitches are about to burst. But this, he rasped, his lung thinking back to the infinite cigarettes he'd consumed in his previous life; this, the pain in your eyes, is just the beginning. You're going to have to keep your head leaning forward so the gas rises, puts pressure on the retina, and the retina scars over. For how long? I asked, not paying much attention, not thinking about the effort it would be for my neck, the tension, the acute kinks I would have. Between four and five weeks, maybe six, said a hesitant and particularly cautious Lekz. The time it will take the gas to dissolve. But five or six weeks will fly by. Fly by, I repeated, rushing ahead without calculating that the brain weighs a kilo and a half, and you had to add the skull on top of that. A dead weight at ninety degrees that I would have to start carrying immediately. You have to keep your head down, ordered Lekz without an ounce of compassion. Lower it now and don't raise it again until the bubbles disappear completely.

my mother's other

That night, my mother left for the airport: her patients were clamoring for her return while that daughter who wanted to stop being a daughter was waiting impatiently for her to leave. Are you going to be ok? asked my mother, assuming my father's voice. Are you going to be ok? embracing me but trying to distance herself. The taxi was waiting by the sidewalk. You're going to be ok, she repeated, somewhere between an affirmation and a question. My head nodded, lolling badly guillotined from my neck. My hands supported it. My mother trembled, while the doctor part of her demanded she get hold of herself, dry her tears on the sleeve of her blouse, not be late for her plane. We have to go, my mother's other was saying, right now; and yes, I thought, both of you go, but especially the doctor you. But my mother closed up like a lock while the other nudged her away from me. She was doubting her decision to leave, my mother, and she still refused to do it for a few more minutes. She fought with herself to keep the other from speculating on what could happen if she left, because the other her was National Champion in Pessimism. If she were to listen, my mother, to the suspicions of the doctor's bleak brain, she would never be able to let me go. No matter how loudly her responsibilities summoned her. Her gravely ill kids and their mothers. Because although she and her other dissented and argued, they always agreed when it came to starring in family tragedies. I'll be ok, mom, you can leave, I insisted, but she squeezed me tighter and when she did I felt, in the wire cage that my ribs had become, how the two of them twisted and struggled. Her bones crunched against mine, her extremities bent, out of proportion. The doctor was still fighting to get away, while my mother clutched me close. And although the sweaty heat of that body in double movement brought on in me a certain aversion and a bit of mistrust, there was also something incomprehensible that kept me from letting her go. The three of us were tangled up in the cord of illness, immersed, all three, in a sticky and amniotic fluid that threatened to drown us. Ignacio came up from behind to impose order on our council. It's time, he said, not offering my mother any option but escape. The luggage is in the trunk, he rushed her along, and the taxi meter is running. The driver was smoking comfortably behind the wheel, very close to us; I could smell the burning tobacco and even his tension. Dear, my mother whispered falteringly, blowing her nose on a tissue rescued from a pocket. Dear, as if in secret, if I could, my dear, and this she said alone, as my mother and no one else: daughter, if I could, I'd give you my eyes. I'd pull them out right here in the street, I'd be delighted for you to have them. I'm old, I've gotten enough use out of them. I hear Ignacio in the background talking to the taxi driver, telling him we were almost ready, and I feel chastised, my head hanging between my shoulders, not knowing what I should say, how to reply, other than to thank her slowly and move away from her suffocating presence. Thanks, but there's no need, I'm going to be fine, sensing in that instant that the doctor in my mother adjusted her glasses and raised her eyebrows and whispered, evilly, how could you think of giving your eyes to anyone, especially this one who doesn't even know how to take care of them. The doctor in my mother reproved her: what would you see your patients with? But I wasn't interested in hearing the two of them argue or criticize each other, the way they'd always done. I was planted on the cement, lingering over the image of my mother plucking out one eye with her long painted nails, and then extracting the other. I was seeing those eyes before me, a bit yellowed now, not so white anymore, very round, attached to the empty cavity by a thick, bright red nerve that stretched and narrowed but didn't break, and while my mother tried to snap it and I yelled formaldehyde! Someone! Formaldehyde! Because eyes are organs that don't last long. Because eyes are the first organ to go bad. (I thought all this trying to stop thinking it, and then I remembered that formaldehyde is only good for preserving dead tissue.) Breaking the doctor's rule, I straightened my neck and planted two kisses on my mother, one on each eyelid, and I left my lips there a moment longer than was appropriate for a daughter's kiss. But that skin was so soft, the warmth so perfect, so tender and slight the movement in the sockets. My mother was no longer hugging me, she slackened her arms, said a friendly goodbye to Ignacio—goodbye, son, she said to him, and I heard her but I found myself thinking, suddenly heartbroken, that those eyes of hers were too fibrous. They were used eyes, worn out and even dilapidated from medicine, too-old eyes, and I pushed my mother toward the taxi door so she would finally leave. And as the car moved away I started to laugh, to laugh slowly, my neck slightly bent, my head conquered, my sight covered, imagining the fright I would give myself if I looked in the mirror with those senile pupils. Then I heard her brittle voice floating back to me as she fled, her voice coming out the window of the moving car, dear, shouted my operatic and visionary mother: my dear daughter, you can count on my eyes, they're yours if you want them.

killing a little

Ignacio ended up with the hair-raising mission of separating my trimmed eyelashes, his fingers like pincers, of attending to my glassy or lifeless gaze, the iris distended in a black hole, the cornea perforated with three badly-sewn stitches and swollen around each pupil. Each eye inflated to the point of bursting, the constant itching of scabs under the skin. It was there that Ignacio had to apply various eyedrops, a series of unguents, and then clean the grease that seeped out along the edges when the eye finally closed, beaten by the mortal weight of the eyelids, patches, and cramps that moved down from my neck to my back. I'm hungry, I announced, while Ignacio washed, disgusted and dizzy and faint, his fingers, hands, nails, elbows, teeth. And though he didn't feel like eating, we ordered sandwiches of bloody meat from the Cuban restaurant on the corner. To get our strength back, I insisted, so we don't go to bed on an empty stomach. But it was another ordeal to eat without raising my head. Lower it, ordered Ignacio, now become the doctor's sassy ventriloquist's doll. You're going to get cataracts, he said, losing patience, furious, livid, exhausted: my nurse. Lower it, he said in a martyr's voice, and the consolation of food started to turn sour. It was hard to chew and dangerous to swallow with my head sunk down. It was impossible to talk without raising my face, my face that regularly defied the order and instinctively straightened to meet a gaze. Eyes never give up, I said. They always seek out other eyes, realizing that was the impulse I was obeying, but Ignacio refused to accept explanations. Lower it. I should speak to him only with words, not eyes. I should control my neck. I should please stop rocking, forward and back, in my chair. Ignoring my will, my mechanical body went on swinging like a pendulum; my head struggled to lift and my eyelids to open, and I scared Ignacio with my moth eyes full of light. Close them, said my nurse, queasy to his core, forcing down a bit of bread and a little water. *Joder de dios*, fucking christ, I can't eat looking at you. Watching over me disturbed him, but neither could he rest at night, keeping vigil over my sleep: every movement of mine kept him from falling asleep. I crashed, defeated by every kind of discomfort and oblivious to the nocturnal position of my head, while Ignacio sat up and shook me to save me from myself. Turn over, you're in a bad position, and he pushed me impatiently into the ideal pose for the bubbles. I didn't remember anything of what happened at night, whether we argued or not, if we kissed or spat on each other, if we desired each other lying one curled around the other or me on his chest, if we killed each other a little more. Ignacio, a professional slave, got up at dawn and made himself a cup of black coffee. Coming and going in the morning fatigue, he said goodbye or got free of me with a slam of the door. It was impossible to keep Ignacio there, make him desist from his daily flight to the office, take him out of his classes, away from all those students who returned his gaze with ambitious insolence. Like a miser, he stashed away the spontaneous laughter and brainy conversations, his lips full of political science, debates, corruption, his lips forgetting me a little, while I rested too from his tantrums, and basked in the minuscule noises the house orchestrated in his absence. But Ignacio's love was spiraling and elastic, it stretched without breaking and brought him back to my side. He called me to be sure I'd gotten out of bed, that I had found the lukewarm coffee on the table and the toast already spread with butter, the syringe at the ready. He wanted to know if I'd gone back down the hallway downcast, if I'd thrown myself face down on the mattress, and how I was keeping my mind entertained. I crawled around the house, giving vague lies as answers to everything or almost everything; yes, yes, I said, hauling around and supporting my punished head, yes standing in front of the refrigerator door, yes sticking a bored finger all the way to the bottom of the food containers, leaving a path of crumbs that later Ignacio—trailing the smell of the city, of open streets and old papers, a smell of happiness that soon dissolved—would have to sweep up. Mop. Gather or clean and scorn me and adore me, giving himself to my desires as if to a vice, without imposing deadlines, Ignacio, or conditions.

flashes, lightning

(To sense or invent the sound of your rhythmic footsteps coming down the hall. Imagine some keys turning in the lock, the tongue of the deadbolt licking inside the door, the touch of shoe soles on the still-bare floorboards over which you tread slowly, looking for me. Lina? I slip away to nooks and crannies of the apartment that I've been training myself to recognize as if I had your myopic eyes, even in your absence. I've stopped limping; the limp tapered off because all the pain slid along my vertebrae toward my neck, toward my face, leaving the rest of my body free: I separate my legs tenuously, I lift my knees laboriously, bend them over my chest, no longer the paralytic blind woman. Lina? Here, I say, in the bedroom. I stretch out in the bed and grow a few centimeters while I bare my thighs. And between Ignacio's repugnance and discouragement, between his smell of hunger and crumpled cigarettes, between my legs. Here. And you accept what I offer you like a famished dog receives its fleshless bone. You seem thinner to me and more miserable, but I've also become more fleshless, meager, faint. We go at each other with our teeth like electric animals, the current of your body revives me, I'm the patched product of your lightning. Sparks fly in my eyes, white and blue sparks like lightning. *Lightning*, I cry, I'm seeing lightning, I tell you, enraptured and amazed, possessed by the terror and the spell, but don't stop, and I bury my nails in your back. It's hallucinatory sex, the sparks flash in every suture of my retina, I want to tell you about it, describe every detail, but you cover my mouth, you stifle my obsession with detail, you need to forget for now, at least for this instant, who we are and what we're doing there, who you are and who you were before. I can't do it with you shouting, and even less when you're laughing so hard. But how long has it been since I've laughed, I reply, since I've laughed like this. Like a lunatic, you answer, wearing an expression that I picture as afraid. Sometimes you scare me, you say, bitter and panting and separating from me as if from a sock full of splinters. Sometimes I don't know who you are in bed. I hardly ever know who you are. Yours is a disconsolate and true voice that suddenly intimidates me. Are you telling me you want to give up? I hear you light a cigarette. We're sprawled on top of the sheet. I'm face up, you're face down. Without raising my head I move closer and ask for a drag. I turn my electrified back to you so your fingers can receive the spark of energy that this moment requires. We reconnect. And then, you say as though continuing an interrupted conversation, one that you've been holding alone for minutes or months; then, when you laugh like that you make me feel like a stranger, like you don't recognize me, like I'm transitory. You make me feel terribly alone. (But that's what we are, two strangers brought together by accident in the impossible riddle of illness.) I don't want to feel alone with you, you say solemnly, because I don't have anyone anymore. I don't have parents, no brothers or sisters, I don't trust my friends anymore. You're the only thing I have, and I'm not even sure of that. What I want to know, you say, is if you're going to leave me when you get better. If you'll abandon me. That is, you say, would you be willing to get married? Get married, I repeat, not understanding the word, married; I'm silent, moved, kneading that resonant and ominous question, hearing the frenetic, delicate wingbeats of that phrase, calculating the implications of the question and the consequences of its answer. It depends, I tell you, in a moment of suspense filled with love and vileness; it depends on how much you love me, on how much more you're willing to do for me.)

dictation

It was one thing to theorize strategies of the subaltern and resistance from the margin, and quite another, radically opposed, to empathize. My colleagues' strategy turned out to be this: turn a blind eye. Take refuge in their reading. Seek protection in the academy and let themselves be tarred by their jargon. What could they tell me, when they only knew how to talk about arduous concepts stuffed in even darker books that I wasn't reading.

Maybe they thought it was impossible to think without eyes. Did they believe that in order to think one had to be up on the latest theory? I never got the chance to tell them that I did nothing but read during my long days of blindness. Every week I received books on tape, kilos on kilos, in the mail. I clung to fiction like I did to Ignacio. Only my thesis advisor knew. Only she bothered to dial my number on occasion. How did your surgery go? asked her dilapidated but firm voice, in which her first accent barely sounded. I don't know what to tell you, I said, and she jumped to the next line without giving me time to share any details, which were now my specialty. Silvina had plenty of details, she was another expert on the horrors of the body. She was a master of survival: in addition to academic diplomas she brandished intangible medals certifying that she'd vanquished death, twice in a row. And your writing? she asked me. How is the writing going? What writing? I asked, reminding her that we'd agreed I would suspend my research. Illness in Latin American literature, I thought, thinking I was like an anthropologist who falls in love with her subject. An excessive, risky love, because my subject has taken me over, has turned against me. And that's when I should have battened the hatches, thrown my thesis overboard. I was doing nothing but plugging novels into my ears or listening to the news on the radio or TV, trying not to disconnect from the world but abstaining from my own writing. I meant, said Silvina, the novel you were writing. The novel, I replied. That shapeless thing is this now, I said, and I was speechless after that phrase that not even I really understood. But you can't stop writing, she urged, write the now, the every day. Write a blind memoir, I said.

Silvina said, there are so many blind writers. There's only one, I reminded her. True, she murmured. And we fell silent, while she thought about that writer and his hourly readers, his successive secretaries and stenographers; I was thinking, meanwhile, about Silvina's trembling hands, the peristaltic movement of her fingers when she talked, the eyelid slightly fallen over her left eye that lent her a disquieting and beautiful affect. But Silvina interrupted our simultaneous thinking, as if she were confirming something. Dictate to a recorder, that's what you have to do: dictate. Dictating a novel isn't the same as listening to them, I told her. Dictate a diary, then, she said. And I told her my impulse had always been toward fiction. It wasn't actual events that drove me, but rather words, and it was my hand that pushed the words, that built them up and then broke them down to forge the phrases again. Writing was a manual exercise, pure juggling. It would be easier to learn braille, which required fingers, than to try to work by ear. But why not try? she asked, resolute. Do you have a recorder? Should I send you mine? You'll get used to it quickly. No, Silvina, I'm not ever going to get used to it and I don't want to, I told her, somber, feeling my reluctant words grating on the silence that came next. You do realize that you're making Lina Meruane disappear? And I, unhesitating, told her that Lina Meruane would come back to life as soon as the blood was in the past and I had my sight again.

mutilated

The cordless phone stayed in my pocket and rang at all hours and I—lying in some part of the house, on the still nonexistent sofa or armchair—on the floor wounded from the move—but most often stretched out on the bed so I could bear the weight of my head, I pressed the button and said simply, yes? Yes? wondering when I would start to say no. It could always be Manuela calling to suggest a visit that I always put off. It could be Ignacio calling from his office or my mother or father or both together from Santiago. My father uttered only a hesitant Lucina? daughter? How are those eyes doing? because right away my mother would snatch the phone away or interrupt from the other extension. Now that there was no one in the house but them, all the phone extensions were available. There was one in every room and they used them all to call me. This time it would be them, I thought, because Ignacio had just left his office. They greeted me simultaneously: how are those eyes doing? My father immediately ran out of questions and ceded the conversation to my mother. And without listening to a single answer about my condition or my apprehension, my mother categorically pinned a weakness on me. I was losing hold of my patience, she said. I was losing confidence and sanity. My whole being was faltering but I had to be strong, because I had the privilege of being alive. I know you're not well, she said. My barometer never fails me, added my fantastic and abrupt mother from eight thousand two hundred and fifty-three kilometers plus a few meters away. Nothing she said worked as consolation. Still doubting, doubting but not controlling herself, she thought—thinking wrong—that a story worse than my own would put things into perspective. Being blind is nothing, nothing, she told me. It's nothing compared to what just happened to this poor medical student. I shouldn't have asked, but I fell into

138

LINA MERUANE

my mother's trap and I did ask about the poor medical student
who I had almost ten years on—nine, exactly. This poor student,
my mother—exaggerated, gloomy, morbid—started to tell me,
had taken the train down south, and in the middle of the night
something crossed her sleeping mind, a bad premonition blowing
smoke and hissing in the darkness of some closed-up station; no
one knows what it was, said my mother, but the student started
to walk through the train in search of her bad luck. And when
crossing between two cars she made a false move that was sadly
far from false, it was a step that dropped her into a void—there
was nothing between the cars, not even a little piece of platform.
My mother paused while both of us thought about her fall onto
the sharp tracks and the indolent train continuing on its way.
Are you there? I'm here, where am I going to go? I said, wishing
I hadn't felt the fall, the student's mortal drubbing. She bled out
and died, right? No, replied my mother. She was unconscious on
the tracks and she woke up when the train had already disappeared.
She didn't know what had happened to her. There was no moon
that night and she couldn't see a thing, she didn't understand
why she couldn't get up, why her hands wouldn't obey her. She
started to shout, because she heard some sleepless dogs barking
in the distance. Until finally the neighbors were alerted by the
barking and ran to help her. Following a mechanical impulse, my
mother tells me then that the train had sliced off both arms and
both legs. And then… she continued, but I already knew where
she was going and I didn't want her to go there, I didn't want her
to torment me any more, never again. Then nothing, I told her.
I don't want to hear any more. I don't want to know. How could

you even think to compare my fate with hers? I asked her, feeling an old rage rising up, a visceral terror that had never really left me; I could forget it, but my mother was always there to bring it back and bully me with her own anxiety. Don't tell me about any more tragedies, Mom, never, ever again. And, pushing all the buttons at once, I cut our communication off for a few days.

double effect

Locked in the bathroom I take off my patches: first one and then the other, and third, I open my eyes. By now the stitches of black thread have broken and fallen out, according to their mysterious design. No longer are there only halos of strident light. By now the bubbles have started to shrink, leaving the edges to my true peripheral vision splashed with tenuous and imprecise colors, residues of a rainbow that will never again have the same brilliance. In the center, though, the gas is a lens, a powerful magnifying lens through which the lines of my hand grow and enlarge when I hold it close, or the tiny flowers pressed into the soap dish, the directions on the aspirin bottle. I have the impression I'm hallucinating. This seems like seeing, but it's much more than seeing, it's having a true bionic eye. Having lost the habit of using my eyes, I feel around in the drawer for a hand mirror. What I see in it, held two centimeters in front of my face, are the holes of my nose and above them two swollen, wounded balls, two open and unfathomable pupils, and if I move away I see my two eyes become four. I inhale and move further away, I check what each eye sees separately and I'm worried when I find that while the right one produces exaggerated and pristine images, the left one perceives things somewhat distorted. I try them together: I see duplicated objects. I think that double as I may be seeing, seeing is the good news; but I see badly, and that's the bad. Then I see two tears on the surface of my mirror, mine and its own carbon copy. Something went wrong, I let Ignacio know when through the keyhole I hear him coming back with a carton of eggs and a box of milk. In this eye, I tell him, some-thing's-wrong, measuring and separating each syllable, there's a problem here, maybe two. What problem, how do you know? he stammers, knowing what this could mean: more operations or the final operation. I see badly and I see double. Double, babbles Ignacio with a dry mouth, confused and sick of surprises but also startled that I could even know I saw badly. Couldn't you be imagining it? (How to explain this to you, who never lived through losing your sight and then seeing again, each eye on its own.) Explanations are too much. My body knows with irrefutable certainty that this is worse than bad. Worse than the aftereffects of the blinding laser Lekz used to gradually burn the inside of my eye over the years. Worse than the swelling of the soft tissues that kept me from reading after his procedures. Worse than the possible tears from the pincers in the operating room, than the tight scabs on my retinas, than the cataracts when the helium finally disappears. I renounce science and its possible explanations. This is an eye giving up, a limping eye, one eye or two that are irreversibly sick. And I let some furious and acid tears fall, and I punish them, my damned eyes, leaving them at the mercy of my hands that peck at them, dig into them, press on them and dry them recklessly. Ignacio tries in vain to stop me.

I lift my chin and I lift my eyelids. I see his two big, terrified bulbs that suddenly become four blurry eyes. (So many eyes, you have more than enough, four eyes with four lenses for myopia.) Let go of me, I tell him harshly, we don't need to play eye doctor, there's no way to win at that game. And as if the devil were listening and wanted prove me right, when I turned my indignant head I slammed it into the door. A violent blow against the handle. A dry and resounding impact that has a devastating effect. Blood, again, in my eye. A fine thread of blood that comes from I don't know where. Another double effect, another copy of what happened before, it's all happening again but this time I start to scream, to cry out and not from pain. Ignacio yells and shouts back at me, what happened? Where did you hit yourself? I have my eyes wide open, I'm watching as the eye watches its thread of blood, looking at everything without ceasing my cries: I'm bleeding I'm bleeding again. But you can't be bleeding, he said, tongue-tied and flustered, you can't bleed anymore, they removed those veins. Then I shout louder, I shout all the shouts I hadn't shouted when I should have. I see red again, Ignacio, I'm seeing blood with my own eyes. (I want to yank out yours, stick them inside mine so you can see the blood. Ignacio runs toward the bedroom to dial Lekz's number. He asks to talk to Doris: yes, Doris, I hear him say, skipping over the greeting, yes Doris, we know Lekz doesn't see patients on the last Friday of the month, we know that's his day off. *¡Que te calles!* And though Doris speaks nothing but English, she understands in the universal language of hysteria that this is a moment for silence. I hear Ignacio give a resonant grunt and then, with his professorial diplomacy, modulating every consonant, every learnedly British syllable, breathing deeply for an instant to recover his tone, please, Doris, put me in touch with Lekz. And he turns to me, standing in the doorway, clutching at myself, and he tells me, panting, get dressed right now, we're going.

setbacks

We raise our arms in the street as if asking for help, but what stops in front of us is a yellow car that takes off like an autumn gale, wildly crossing the city on the highway. Ignacio hands the driver some warm and crinkly bills and we storm in and sit down. Ignacio notes right away that the clientele today is different; Fridays at noon are when they schedule operations with the cataract specialist. They're all patched like me—because I've put my patches back on—but they hold their heads high and proud like fighting cocks. I hear a well-known clucking coming closer. It's Doris, who kneels down beside me and brings her greasy lips close to my ear to announce: we have a setback. Yes, I repeat, we do, or more like I do. Doris nods and asks if they've contacted me as well. Who are they? The company! What company? I say gloomily; I certainly want no company other than Ignacio's. Doris, who doesn't know how to attend to more than one office problem at a time, sits ruminating for a second, confused by my confusion, her gaze fixed on some documents until the mystery is resolved and she finds herself with the need to clarify that, right now, this isn't about me. But for some time now everything has seemed to be about me. But no, says Doris again, forget about yourself and your eyes for two minutes. Doris wants to talk to me,

143

but I feel like there's no more room inside me, not for any more air or blood or any more bureaucracy, and I'm going to explode while she talks about the damned insurance company. They don't want to pay for the operation. My operation, I say to myself without contradicting her, but noting that once again we are talking about my body. The company, Doris continues with a brittle air, approved an operation that wasn't the one you ended up having. Things got complicated in the operating room. Oh, really? I say just to say something, trying to reroute my thoughts toward some zone of my existence that doesn't entail complication, but I can't find any. Yes, says Doris, unable to bear the weight of her own body, slowly gets up and sits on a chair next to us. Yes, she says, the company determined that your tests don't contain conclusive evidence of any defect or lesion or visual anomaly. And since I'm no longer answering, she is the one who asks the usual rhetorical questions and then responds to them. What did they want? she exclaims, a blind woman with a cane and a guide dog to confirm the operation was absolutely unavoidable? My operation, I think in secret, what would it cost her to say it's mine, just like my tests, my life, my Ignacio. Ignacio stays silent, determined to not get up from the chair again, and the two of us follow his example, all three of us silent, all three of us glum, our legs crossed, each stringing together various ideas around that millionaire figure that could be for nothing, that the insurance is refusing to pay. But the battle-hardened secretary can't bear her silence for long, and she abandons it to tell me how they're some real good-for-nothings, and it's not the first time they've done this to us. We'll send them the video of the operation (*my* operation, mine and maybe a little bit yours, Ignacio), along with a box of popcorn, she goes on. We'll swamp them with photographs blown up and framed to make them understand, and full copies of all your records, we'll send them all the most recent medical literature, the research protocols, we'll bombard them with emails. Doris promises to bombard them with calls, overwhelm their phones. Until they get sick of me, she concludes, anticipating victory. They'll pay us every last penny. Don't let them scare you. And giving little pats to my hand she gets up laboriously, making the chair creak. As she leaves us she greets Lekz, who is arriving just then, his hair slicked back by the wind. Good afternoon, he says, and his expression when he sees us is puzzled.

recognition

Lucina, I said to him, and I reached out my hand to the air and to him, because I knew he'd already forgotten me. He always forgot, in spite of our unhappy and almost historic adventures through consulting and operating rooms. Lucina, doctor, I know you won't remember, I said, promising myself I would make him remember me. Lowering his voice impossibly, Lekz asked me to forgive him, it wasn't me he forgot. It was everyone. Much as he struggled, he watched them enter his office and he didn't have the slightest idea who they were, that's what he told me, clearing his throat continuously, the magnifying lens raised before my eyes but still without examining me. With his hand suspended in the air, he confessed that patient after patient would come in and he would greet them all by name, something he'd learned to do mechanically.

Greeting them as though he knew them was part of the job. A matter of checking the list that the diligent Doris left typed up for him on the table. Hi Peter. Step inside, Gary. How are you, Ms. Smith, nice to see you. And so they went, entering one after the other, to detail their optical difficulties: one hemorrhage, torn retina, glaucoma, or macular degeneration after another. Such everyday things that they gradually became indistinguishable. After so many years, the names became insufficient too. They don't say anything to me anymore, he said, effortlessly raising his thick gray eyebrows, wrinkling his brow, aging a century. Their voices say absolutely nothing to me, their faces either. They talked without seeing him, I thought, he looked at their faces without recognizing them. They all seemed discreetly familiar, each one of their gestures, their inflections, generated a fleeting glimmer, a pulsation, a throbbing in the cerebral cortex that never congealed into a memory. Nor did the clinical histories tell him anything, because he was unable to decipher his hieroglyphical notes from previous visits. Like an illiterate lost in an excess of signals, he faced them all, every day. But he sat them down and his lens prepared to read the full story of every eye. On that surface each patient's identity was revealed to him: as he peered into them, he remembered details. He even remembered the order of his enlightenments. But no, it's not remembering, Lekz specified as he instructed me to lean my head back; it's not exactly looking back or recalling. Lean further, he repeated, forcing his voice while he lifted my eyelid to begin the exam and immerse himself in my wide, dilated pupil. It's not a memory, it's recognition. Because inside, but also outside, all the eyes were different and now they all had his signature.

In spite of the emergency, Lekz sounded faraway when he repeated his passwords: up, first, up and to the right, to the side. All the way. A little down and now all the way down. My neck turned ritually on its axis. And following that circular tour, Lekz lit up the whole perimeter of my retina with that strongest of all magnifiers. I waited for him to tell me what he saw there, what image of me was emerging from the depths of my eye. What did his diagnosis say about my life? What's happening with my eyes, doctor? Ah, he said, lengthening the *a* in the voice of an oracle or iridologist or simply a charlatan oculist. These retinas are my masterpiece.

veins

But your artwork came out crooked, I said, exasperated but above all astonished at what he hadn't seen. Crooked? You didn't look hard enough, doctor. Lekz cleared his throat as if his years as a smoker were handing him the bill right there. It's another hemorrhage. Don't worry, muttered Lekz uneasily, grabbing a handful of his hair and pulling at it gloomily; bleeding a little isn't so strange after an operation, he said. It's nothing unusual, he repeated, there's no cause for alarm. He insisted on calm, talking between his teeth before falling silent, shielded by his magnifying lens. His was not just any silence; it was a silence that emanated from his body. Lekz had stopped breathing. I had also given up on breathing. I was deciding to suffocate myself. It was so much silence that we—and not only us, the people in the waiting room, too—could have disintegrated, the world could have disappeared and taken Ignacio with it. I thought of him with dismay, I wondered about his anxious decision to stay outside. He'd announced it firmly, though at the last second he changed his mind and walked to the door with us. Lekz closed the door in his face. Ignacio must have returned to his chair; he'd be feverishly turning pages of magazines without paying an ounce of attention. Lekz separated his lips, his mouth sucked in air and inflated his infirm lungs, and he interrupted my silence with his words. There's been a slight flaw. A flaw or a surprising imperfection, it's true, he admitted. I don't know how I didn't see it before now, he murmured with premonitory bitterness. He was so close I could hear his nails scratching his neck, the vein throbbing at his throat. He took off the metal headlamp and explained falteringly that he'd left some ringleted veins uncut, some veins just in the center of the left eye. I left them there, he repeated, punishing himself with the repetition. I was convinced that. I thought. Maybe he was lying to himself and rubbing his eyelids, maybe it was true that in those hours he'd gotten all the veins. And if these were new ones? Veins from these past few days? Lekz was more alone, tenser and darker than his own shadow. I've never seen this before, but it's possible one of my colleagues has. Or several. Or all of them. They can take a look at you. Our clinical meeting is this afternoon. That way we can be sure. I studied his post-Soviet grimace with my double and wobbly vision while he told me that I wouldn't be asleep, only stunned with a touch of anesthesia. You won't feel a thing, he promised, while he peered out into the waiting room and asked Doris to reserve a time in operating room four. You're going to operate on her right now, doctor? said Doris in a sigh, although on the inside what she did was moo over the accumulation of simultaneous tasks.

But she was a woman trained to moo at the world and lick the hand of a single man, her owner. Right now, Doris, the clinical operating room, bring in the associates for an outpatient check-up, murmured Lekz with the gentleness of all true masters.

disappearances

The city disappears, the hospital opens its doors and I disappear too, without saying goodbye to anyone amid its forms and florescent-lit hallways. This time I have an express ticket, and I use it to enter an operating room stuffed full of eye doctors of varying sizes and shapes, all distorted and a little double. I can halfway make out when Lekz appears in his green suit among the others wearing the same disguise. I halfway realize that they've all finished their morning surgeries but have stuck around to witness, along with Lekz, the mystery of my veins. I also half-hear their anecdotes, their condolences, their political comments, but I feel nothing. Nothing, either, when they announce the hit of liquid anesthesia. I only ask that the effect last longer than this collective violation, and much as I hate being manhandled, I decide to give in. I close my eyes for an instant so Lekz can open them again for me in a little while. And now they're open, little by little. I hear other people's voices, nearby conversations that I retain but only halfway. Someone utters the word vein and someone else repeats it until they make it disappear. Someone uses the word proliferation. Someone uses the phrase hormone-aided growth. If she was a man this wouldn't have happened. I know that someone else peers over me and I think something about something, but what?

There are bloody words everywhere. I know they are discussing my fate but I know I'm not sure what they've decided, and a sip of water reaches my mouth in the recovery room and then tea and bland crackers in a common room full of people. There are no eye doctors, no nurses, no Ignacio. I'm waiting for him to appear and go home with me. They won't let me leave on my own, I could keel over, I could sue them for damages; I'll have to stay here another night because Ignacio has disappeared. He's not going to come tonight. Maybe not tomorrow. You're never going to come back, Ignacio, is what I say to myself before my blackout.

eye for an eye

I opened my eye, and there was the little girl with the patch over one side of her face, the girl shooting the electric ray of her gaze at me. In that single uncovered eye is concentrated all the fear of hospitals that now falls like an ax onto my cornea. While outside the street revives—a gust or a whisper in the distance—and the sun peers indignantly through the gaps in the curtains to track us with its flame; while light bulbs swayed slightly in the ceiling, moved by the incessant march of Filipinas changing shifts; while I struggled to wake up, the dazzling, chilling blue of her eye had already been awake for hours, aimed at me. I half-closed my own eye, trying to protect myself. (I looked for you, but you hadn't appeared.) I blinked, unable to convince myself that I'd emerged from an anesthetic void only to fall, struck down by the gaze of a little girl who was waiting for her doctor too. The creature didn't take her eye off me, didn't hold back a gram of that pupil. It was her eye against mine, but mine was just an iris tattered by operations, a faltering pupil. Was she a demon, a sprite, a post-op hallucination? At what point had this girl arrived, so little and so bewildered at finding another cyclops like herself? She was a couple meters away, perplexed; she didn't complain or scratch at the skin around her patch, and I looked away. And in that deflection that was the only possible escape, I realized the little girl wasn't alone. No. Around the girl were clamped the fingers of someone who must be her mother. Don't stare at her like that, murmured the woman, and her voice echoed off the room's high ceilings. Don't look at her, she's looking at you, she repeated, though without the slightest modesty she brazenly ran her own eyes over me: both of hers staring at my lack of one. It's not polite, she explained, though still blasting me with her gaze. My naked eye was looking at the blurry girl, and then the mother, who was wiping the oil from her forehead, and then at the daughter, confused, waiting for something to happen. Have they taken one of your eyes too, I heard the mother say. Did they have to cut out a cancer. It wasn't a question but rather a recrimination, a reproach that the mother unsheathed to show that her suffering was superior, the suffering of a mother facing her daughter's single but devastating eye. And then I remembered my mother, my mother thrusting her old eyes on me as we said goodbye, and I thought about Ignacio, his two flawless black eyes, his eyes he didn't seem aware of; and I also thought I would be left very alone without my eye if I lost it; I'd have an orphan face. And then. If you care so much about your daughter, ma'am, I said, challenging her, daring her to a duel with herself. If the loss hurts you that much, give her the eye that she's missing. Give it to her right now, though it's still too big for her.

proof

(I know that you were committing a slow suicide by nicotine while our fate was being decided. The hours passed by you and you didn't see them, Ignacio, nor did you see the nurses or the janitors mopping under your feet. You didn't see anything until you saw Lekz saying goodbye to the court of eye doctors and walking desolately down a hall. His face was shrouded, his arms hung burdened and lifeless by his sides, and Lekz told you we'll talk tomorrow, we'll talk about everything, with Lucina, more calmly. For now it's best you take her home, and you get some rest too, he said, avoiding your name. And he said goodbye without looking at you, leaving you standing in the air, suspended, with the chance for a sudden but maybe premeditated escape, the guilty flight that would one day bring you tamely back. You had nowhere to go, I had become your only place, you told me all this later, don't you remember? How you felt the need to flee. You went out to buy another pack of cigarettes, to walk through the warm night that suddenly smelled to you like violets, and you walked away following that scent like a goose chasing spring, but the violets disappeared from the breeze and suddenly you were in a square planted with weeds and soulless benches frequented by ruined old men in pants that no one washed, old men who slept alone, each by himself under cardboard sheets until the snow, the

ice came, and then. Then? You said aloud, but no one heard your
question because you were alone. Like the old man you would
soon be, in the future, thinking about that girlfriend you'd abandoned in the hospital, erupting in blood. And then nothing, you
shouted, terrified of your own howl, suspicious of the anguished
murmur you heard. Were they yours, all those voices arguing sav-
agely inside you? Was it true, had Lucina or her voice really said
that to you before she went into surgery? You shook your head,
no, it's not true, then nothing, nothing, you repeated like crazy, but
the voice pecked at your head, it wouldn't let you erase the words
I had thrown at you only a few hours before, my voice asking
for that, the ancient proof of love. Only one, Ignacio, the proof is
only one, I would never ask for both. The smallest proof I could
ask you for, scarcely larger than a marble. I asked you because
I had no choices left, because I had understood even before Lekz
did that all his science had failed. It's not true, you told yourself,
and you repeated that our conversation had not happened, that
I would never have dared, ever, but then you started to think
otherwise, that I *had* asked you for something you held so dear,
and my request was so vivid, so exact, so simple, that you couldn't
have made it up. Which of us is crazier, you asked, and I know you
let out a peal of dry laughter trying to think of something other
than my voice, something beyond me; you went on repeating with
sudden happiness that the thing you would give me would unite
us forever, it would make us equal, turn us into mirror images
for the rest of our lives until death. And even after, my voice told
you in your head, though we knew nothing about after. What
matters is now, that's what I'd told you, turning my face away

when you wanted to put an end to the discussion. Put an end to it as though it had never happened. But what the fuck are you asking me for, Lucina, you asked me, blaring your voice in the park, talking to the air and the rats, the pigeons. How could you even think I'm going to give you that, you said, without daring to name what I was asking for. Just *that*. But how could you think of that, you said in silence, kicking some burned sticks with rage, with justified distrust, suddenly wondering, jealously, if there was another man who could say yes, yes, Lucina, yes, I do want to be yours forever. A guy capable of saying it and feeling it literally. I know that you were tortured by your own indecision, your difficulty in answering my request with a round yes or an equally definitive no. Listen to me, Ignacio, I'd said. Don't you think I'd do the same for you? My question resounded, it echoed back to you, it filled your mouth with retching, with bile—because you'd gone hours without eating—empty vomit just imagining that you would give me *that* and you'd have to live looking at me afterward. And you went on killing yourself with puffs of smoke while I slept, strangely tranquil, dreaming of your myopic and beautiful gaze, dreaming free of that shameless question that now you shouldered in the night. I only ask for one. Lenses won't help me, colored glass is worthless. You tried not to think about that, you directed your attention to the flame of the match, you counted how many seconds it took to cool and how long your finger could stay pressed against its ember. I know you tried to empty your mind, staring at those skeletal trees that one by one were losing their leaves in the wind, and there you still were at dawn, going in circles around the square and in your head, wishing I hadn't given you that condition when I said good-bye. If you can't commit and give me what I want, don't come back tomorrow.)

stop

Behind an Ignacio steeped in the smell of cigarettes came Lekz, like an aseptic and pallid angel, suddenly gray, exhausted circles under his eyes. He did not look good. Am I going to die, doctor, or are you? Lekz made an awkward and resigned grimace. I fuzzily saw him lower his face and swell up with air. He would wait outside with Ignacio while I got out of bed and got dressed. And in the minutes that passed while I pulled up my skirt over my dirty underwear, put on my sweaty socks, my boots, pulled on my undershirt, scarf, sweater, and my anxiety over the verdict, I watched an infinite number of treasured and uneven memories parade before my sick eyes, memories of the times when I'd pretended my illness didn't exist, moments that were falsely happy when I'd made myself think I could be someone else; they'd debilitated me and left me at the mercy of an estranged solitude that was mine alone. And I came out with my head high, ready to hear what Lekz had to tell me in the little office the hospital ceded us. The doctor cleared his throat more than ever. Lekz and Ignacio cleared their throats and I did too, it was contagious; I cleared my throat before singing to them, coldly, I'm ready, I'm all ears. I saw Lekz knead his head with all his fingers. I saw him rub his face, not knowing how to explain to me but resolved, no beating around the bush now, like a teletype machine, like he was reading a telegram. There are veins in your left eye. Stop. They're new ones. Stop. Soon they will break the retina. Stop. For now the other eye is calm, but the blood is going to come back. Stop. You'll be blind in no time. Stop. It was definitive. The blood, its possibilities, they had never really disappeared. They were part of my eyes. I felt Ignacio's sweaty hand sliding over mine, Ignacio as a whole seeping away toward the floor. Ignacio now an insane color. Ignacio, I told him, leave me alone for a moment with the doctor. And when I heard the door close I leaned my elbows on the tiny, reeking table, I leaned forward and I told Lekz to light a cigarette for me. I know you smoke in secret, hiding it from your wife, from your patients, and most of all from Doris, hiding from yourself. I can smell the tobacco on your breath. Don't say anything, and I'll keep quiet too. Anyway, it doesn't make sense to try to stop the destruction of my eyes anymore. Lekz opened an invisible little drawer and handed me a cigarette. He lit another one for himself, almost grateful to share his secret. I saw the blurry reflection of the lit end lighting up his eyes in the desolation of that Saturday. I saw my own puffs of ghostly smoke in the air while I thought about how to put it. We only have a transplant left, doctor, you owe it to me. Transplant, repeated Lekz in an agonized voice. Transplant, Lina, he mumbled, no longer doubting my name, and he added a couple of words that got tangled up on his tongue. A transplant is very delicate, he told me, but he was talking to himself in that solemn tone of his. Really very delicate, he said, as though I didn't know. It's only been tried on animals, never on humans. Doctor, I retorted, and I leaned so close to him my smoke burned his cheeks, I'm nothing but an animal who wants to stop being one. Lekz lit a new cigarette on the old one and, opening my file, thumbing through the infinite pages of my history, making a morose doodle around my ever-shorter name, he told me no. It wasn't possible, he said. There were no eye banks, because no one donated dead eyes. It was believed, said Lekz, that memory lived in them, that the eyes were an extension of the brain, the brain peering out through the face to grasp reality. Some people thought the eyes were depositories of memory, he said, and others still believed that the soul was hidden there. It's my only chance, I interrupted, and he was wasting time that I needed; my chance and yours, doctor. I stood up, squinted my eyes so he would feel like I was looking at him, that I wasn't going to allow him anything but an immediate yes. Lekz looked at me in shock, his lips trembled, full of words that now he didn't even dare to think. He cowered down a little in his chair. I heard his fingers drumming somewhere. Lekz was gathering a slow courage in that office, so silent in spite of the sound of the cars crossing the city. The world was so silent, I thought, Lekz so hushed in spite of his nervous fingers, Ignacio so lost in some hallway, pacing anxiously, Chile so far away and mute. And that's what I was thinking when I found myself saying to him, illuminated, electrified, unsteady but sure of what was going to happen. Don't move, doctor, I whispered. Wait for me here, I'll bring you a fresh eye.

LINA MERUANE is one of the most prominent and influential female voices in Chilean contemporary literature. A novelist, essayist, and cultural journalist, she is the author of numerous short stories that have appeared in various anthologies and magazines in Spanish, English, German, and French. She has also published a collection of short stories, *Las Infantas* (Chile 1998, Argentina 2010), a book of essays, *Viral Voyages* (Palgrave, 2014), as well as three novels in addition to *Seeing Red: Póstuma* (2000), *Cercada* (2000) and *Fruta Podrida* (2007). The latter won the Best Unpublished Novel Prize awarded by Chile's National Council of Culture and the Arts in 2006. She won the Anna Seghers Prize, awarded to her by the Akademie der Künste, in Berlin, Germany in 2011 for her entire body of written work. Meruane received the prestigious Mexican Sor Juana Inés de la Cruz Prize in 2012 for *Seeing Red*. Meruane has received writing grants from the Arts Development Fund of Chile (1997), the Guggenheim Foundation (2004), and National Endowment for the Arts (2010). She received her PhD in Latin American Literature from New York University, where she currently serves as professor of World and Latin American Literature and Creative Writing.

MEGAN McDOWELL is a literary translator of many modern and contemporary South American authors, including Alejandro Zambra, Arturo Fontaine, Carlos Busqued, Álvaro Bisama, and Juan Emar. Her translations have been published in *The New Yorker*, *McSweeney's*, *Words Without Borders*, *Mandorla*, and *VICE*, among others. She lives in Santiago, Chile and New York.